Praise for Kirsty Logan

'In her inimitable style, Kirsty Logan explores both the power of refusal and the wild, sharp, unruly edges of women's desire. *No & Other Love Stories* is a dark delight, steeped in blood-red honey'
Heather Parry, author of *Orpheus Builds a Girl*

'An unsettling collection from one of the sharpest, strangest short-story writers working today'
Alice Slater, author of *Death of a Bookseller*

'Absolutely obsessed. Savage, strange and spicy, *No & Other Love Stories* is a fearsome and tart collection of short stories that will devour you whole'
Lucy Rose, author of *Lamb*

'No one writes about the horrific and the erotic, and the tangled up intersections of both, like Kirsty Logan. This book will make you sweat'
Anna Bogutskaya, author of *Feeding The Monster*

'Darkly graceful, innovative, sexy and funny. Kirsty Logan is a jewel'
Camilla Grudova, author of *The Doll's Alphabet*

'Highly original . . . set in a haunting sea-world both familiar and mysterious'
Ursula K. Le Guin

'Mesmerising and evocative'
Observer

'Gripping and unnerving . . . you won't put it down'
Sunday Telegraph

'A dark conjuring of a book: angry, powerful, hypnotic, told in prose of dazzling power'
Kiran Millwood Hargrave, author of *The Mercies*

'Powerful, imaginative, compelling – this is myth-making at its best'
Val McDermid

'A deeply, deeply unsettling and brilliant collection of short stories. Some feature horror, nearly all feature dread and, in the manner of Shirley Jackson, all will burrow their way into your brain and not let go'
Stylist

'Shimmers with menace... Fans of Angela Carter and Shirley Jackson take note' *i*

'Exquisite... uncanny... beautifully compelling'
Roxane Gay

'Logan observes modern anxieties and commonplace troubles and twists them into surreal new shapes... marvellously unnerving... her sharp wit is unmistakable'
New Statesman

'Her poetic, supernatural prose has lace edges of sticky, violent terror... Logan masters the format indubitably, channelling the spirit of Angela Carter... these tales seem to perfectly suit the unsettling times in which we live. Luckily for us, in writing these terrifying tales Logan, like Margaret Atwood or George Orwell, turns the big light on'
Herald

NO & OTHER LOVE STORIES

Also By Kirsty Logan

The Rental Heart and Other Fairytales
The Gracekeepers
A Portable Shelter
The Gloaming
Things We Say in the Dark
Now She Is Witch

No & Other
Love Stories

KIRSTY LOGAN

Harvill
Secker

1 3 5 7 9 10 8 6 4 2

Harvill Secker, an imprint of Vintage, is part of
the Penguin Random House group of companies

Vintage, Penguin Random House UK, One Embassy Gardens,
8 Viaduct Gardens, London SW11 7BW

penguin.co.uk/vintage
global.penguinrandomhouse.com

Penguin
Random House
UK

First published by Harvill Secker in 2025

Typeset in 10.3/18.2pt Ashbury Light by Jouve (UK), Milton Keynes
Printed and bound in Great Britain by Clays Ltd, Elcograf S.p.A.

The authorised representative in the EEA is Penguin Random House Ireland, Morrison
Chambers, 32 Nassau Street, Dublin D02 YH68

A CIP catalogue record for this book is available from the British Library

ISBN 9781787304444

Penguin Random House is committed to a sustainable future
for our business, our readers and our planet. This book is made
from Forest Stewardship Council® certified paper.

For M, because you are 2 and your favourite word is 'no'.

Contents

Piglet

ireille first caught sight of the man through the window of the butcher's shop. The various meats hanging there framed him perfectly, standing in his striped apron, wielding his cleaver. She had never desired anyone or anything as much. He was a beast without beauty, a frog enchanted ugly, a boar-bear-pig thing inexplicably wearing the clothes of a man. His hands were rough-cut wedges of ham, his arms beefsteak. All his features were too big: his nose was bulbous, his eyes bulged like a toad's, his lips were wide and pale like slugs. His visible skin was as red and broken as fresh crackling. His hidden skin, Mireille imagined, was as smooth and white as the fat layered beneath it.

Mireille didn't know the man's real name, and later, when she found out, she didn't care. By then she'd already named him Monsieur Porcine. An invented identity was sometimes better than reality; she knew this from her own life. It had been fine to be a sweet, chubby girl called Mary, but to be a sweet, chubby woman was to be invisible, and that was not fine. So she had become Mireille instead. Mireille was beautiful. To be beautiful, a woman only had to look small and stupid, but not too stupid (there was no such thing as too small). A woman

1

should be small enough that a man can fit his hands around her waist; small enough that she has to stand on her tiptoes to be kissed. But parts of her must be voluptuous; specific parts in isolation from each other. Mireille knew that if someone were to strip her all away, all the parts she'd earned and bought – the lips, the thighs, the hair – she'd be nothing. Not striking, not handsome. Not even ugly. Not remarkable in any way. A pretty-ish female whose looks would soon fade. Utterly worthless.

Through the butcher's window, Mireille watched as Monsieur Porcine lifted his enormous blade and dropped it with incredible force. The cleaver hit the meat with a thud so huge it shuddered the glass of the window. Mireille felt an answering beat between her legs.

That night, in the blank hours when she'd eaten her supper of leaves (no dressing) but it was too soon to go to bed, Mireille opened her laptop. She couldn't stop thinking about Monsieur Porcine and his meaty arms. She googled photos of meat, but that wasn't it. She was hungry for something but didn't know what – except that wasn't quite true because the websites she ended up visiting were very specific. She'd have thought a special browser would be needed to access these sorts of websites, but apparently not. Perhaps it was because most of them were text-based; that way a person could argue that it was all merely fiction, and so be free of any sort of prosecution.

Mireille spent hours on the websites. She read a lot of stories, then graduated to pictures. Her favourites were the illustrations (she didn't like the photographs because it was too apparent that they weren't her), and she enjoyed one illustration in particular: a woman in a huge cauldron, her ankles and wrists bound together with string like a chicken ready for roasting. Presumably as a nod to seasoning, there were carrots, with the leafy tops still attached, looking very much like Mireille's own dinner, inserted into the woman's mouth and vagina. She stared at the drawing for a long time. Then she saved it to her laptop and shut the lid.

It was not that she wanted a carrot in her vagina.

It was that she wanted Monsieur Porcine to put one there.

The next night, despite herself, Mireille found herself visiting the same websites again. Some of the stories Mireille read there began with the getting of the meat: the stalking, the kidnap, the tenderising rape. She skipped those parts. Some of them ended with the actual butchering and eating. She skipped those parts too. She wanted only the prepping and the cooking, the hint of a taste, just to check the flavour. She wanted only the middle, the fatty glorious middle, bound and bulging and bursting, juices dripping, tied and wriggling on a spit, a man watching, his fat hands caressing his own fat belly as his fat tongue licked his fat lips, and the thought of his pink peeping tongue always did it for her, made her imagine his fat pink penis, little mushrooms of his body parts emerging, his lust for her, uncontrolled, beastly, all for her, just for her, and she came so hard she cried out, wordless, animal, as she imagined Monsieur Porcine's meaty hands all over her body, squeezing, slipping, forcing into anywhere he could make his fat fingers fit.

For the next fortnight she followed her new routine: she walked very slowly past Monsieur Porcine's shop, then ate her leaves and looked at the websites and came hard. But it was not enough. She wanted the real thing. She wanted meat meat meat. But she didn't want to eat it; she wanted to be it.

When she began in earnest to seduce Monsieur Porcine, Mireille was surprised at how difficult it was. All men desired her, and he was a man. But perhaps he was more beast than she'd thought. She'd hoped that merely walking into his shop, rather than passing by outside, would be enough to make him drop his cleaver and turn to her instead. But he smiled and greeted her as if she were any other customer. She smiled back, suddenly unsure of herself, and stuttered out an order.

She bought several kinds of meat over several different days before settling on an order of tongue, hoping it would make Monsieur Porcine think of pressing his own fat pink tongue to her soft parts, but he wrapped it in paper and handed it to her with a polite nod. She fed the tongue to stray animals on the way home, to the dogs and cats that convened at her balcony, begging for blood all night. She dreamt of wolves and pigs eating one another, of her tongue growing huge and slipping out of her mouth like a cow's, of Monsieur Porcine buying her and making her clean him with her big cow's tongue like they were both cats.

But her favourite dream – which could more accurately be called a fantasy, as it arose in her waking hours, and only followed her into her sleep because she thought about it so much – took place at the butcher's shop. It was a long and elaborate vision which began with her lying naked on the stainless-steel counter and Monsieur Porcine standing above her. He was silent, appreciative, merely looking. She was cold on the counter and her nipples were as hard as gristle, grown purple in the chilled air. Then, gently, Monsieur Porcine took a pen and marked out her body into different cuts of meat. He sticky-taped little price tags onto the different parts, quantifying the loin and the breast, the flank and the sweetmeats. She could see from the numbers that she was worth a lot. The smaller the quantity of meat, the rarer it was; the more valuable. Finally, Monsieur Porcine placed sprigs of parsley into her mouth and vagina, to show how she might be served, and laid her out in the window display. But the window display did not face out into the street, as they usually did. It faced inwards, so only Monsieur Porcine could see. She was laid out, perfect, precious and priced, ready for him to eat.

Though the seduction took all her skill and much longer than she anticipated, eventually Mireille succeeded, and she and Monsieur Porcine married. When she said her vows she used his real name, but in her head she still called him Monsieur Porcine. They fucked, a lot. She didn't tell him about the websites or her fantasy. She worked the front counter at the butcher's shop. Their profits tripled, even on tripe. There was something undeniably appealing about a tiny and beautiful woman handling large quantities of meat. Sometimes she even let herself make a small surprised gasp, mouth red and round like a vintage pin-up, when the string of sausages spilled out of the machine and into her hands. Their sausages weren't even that good, but they sold a lot of them.

Monsieur Porcine stayed fat and red. Mireille stayed small and beautiful. It was boring and tiring to stay that way, eating leaves and going for long-distance runs every night before bed, but what choice did she have? She had to stay tiny. She couldn't let herself get big and invisible. And every night when Monsieur Porcine climbed on top of her and slid his meaty parts inside her, she knew it was worth it.

One day, Mireille fell ill and took to her bed. Monsieur Porcine brought her a punnet of grapes and a new paperback of a classic novel, the latter being a thing that people always say they'll read while ill in bed but never do. He cleared away her snotty tissues and brought her the washing-up bowl when she thought she might vomit. Mireille filled the room with her stale exhalations. By the time she was better, her hair was slick with oil, spots bracketed her nose and all the polish had chipped off her nails. That night she reached for Monsieur Porcine, and he came to her and kissed her on the mouth, although she hadn't brushed her teeth for two days. She came hard, as she always did with Monsieur Porcine, and fell into a dreamless sleep.

The next morning, Mireille sat up in bed and realised a terrible thing. It was so terrible that she felt dizzy and had to lie down again. Last night she had been disgusting with sickness. But was Monsieur Porcine disgusted? No, he was not. Monsieur Porcine did not desire her because she was small and perfect and beautiful. He did not even merely desire her. He loved her.

Mireille did not know if she loved Monsieur Porcine. But she did want to fuck him, now and always. He was the most alluring creature she had ever seen. But if he was more beast than man, and also alluring, then could the same be true – Mireille was so horrified by this question that now she slid off her bed and lay on the floor – could it be true for her?

It was fine for a man to be a beast: a butcher, an ogre, a thing of meat and lust with fur and fangs and claws, a huge and muscled enemy commander who women ran from, shrieking, but then went home and wrote romance novels about. But men did not write novels about she-beasts. And if they did, the beasts were still tiny and had tits. She did not see how she could take him as he took her.

The years passed, and Mireille and Monsieur Porcine still fucked a lot. She didn't visit the websites again, though she did think about them regularly. She found that her butcher fantasy was creeping back into her life; but this time, instead of imagining herself as the meat, she was the butcher. A few times, while thinking about it at the shop, she managed to bring herself to orgasm while standing at the counter, thighs squeezing and buttocks pulsing, occasionally twisting her body in a way that made the fabric of her bra pull pleasingly on her nipples. She stayed silent when she came, and kept smiling and serving customers, and she didn't mess up a single order.

Monsieur Porcine did mess up the orders. He had something on his mind. He loved the way that he and Mireille fucked, but for him something was, perhaps, a little lacking. No, that was too strong a sentiment; Mireille was complete, but Monsieur Porcine felt the lack in himself.

Before marrying, Monsieur Porcine had run the shop himself. He'd lifted his cleaver high with his powerful arm and thudded it down much harder than necessary, just to show he could. He'd smiled at customers, passed the time of day, allowed them to see how the impressive bulk of him filled the space behind the counter. He'd been on full display at all times, framed by the meat in the window in a way that was not accidental. Monsieur Porcine, after all, had arranged the meat himself.

But now, all anyone saw was Mireille. He could pick her up with his pinkie, and yet she blocked him from view entirely. He did not want to be without Mireille, but sometimes he felt that she was consuming him.

Mireille, as it turned out, really did love Monsieur Porcine. She'd have loved him even if he suddenly became tiny and beautiful. She knew this because when he told her how he felt, her first response was not disgust, which was what she'd expected she'd feel if Monsieur Porcine ever showed her any weakness. Instead she felt sadness, and regret, and a rush of tenderness and panic that she could only describe as love.

That night, after the shop had closed for business, Mireille wrapped herself in Monsieur Porcine's apron. He was much too large to lie up on the counter, so she scrubbed the floor clean enough to eat your dinner off, and he lay there instead. Mireille was silent, appreciative, merely looking. She saw him without his clothes on every night, but this felt different: he was pure meat, pure spectacle. He was for looking at, for salivating over, for making designs on.

She took a pen and marked out his body into different cuts of meat. She sticky-taped on the price tags. She placed sprigs of parsley on his nipples and testicles.

Standing there, looking down at her husband, she felt something under her apron. A pressing, an insistent growth. She knew without looking what it was: a pig tail, pretty and pink, thrusting out from the cleaving of her buttocks.

Later she would lay Monsieur Porcine out just like this in their bed, climb on top, and show him.

Honey

Sigrid's headphones have a buzz in one ear. She's told the tech several times but he hasn't replaced them. Well, never mind, she'll just tell him again. Sweetly, in honeyed tones. A slight smile to show that she doesn't think it's his fault, not really.

'Frank?' she says into the mic. No reply. 'Frankie?' She takes a breath, adds sweetness, unclenches her jaw. They're all in this together, aren't they? She's just like him, her marriage is just as valid as his, she'll be just as much a parent to her wife's baby as he is to his children. 'F-dog?'

'Yo,' he replies immediately, and she dies, actually feels a part of her physical self wither to nothing, at the ludicrous 2004 sub-Limp Bizkit nickname he chose himself, actually chose his own self and now gets people to call him. Half the time she can't even get people to call her Sigrid, which is her *actual name* – she gets Sarah, Simone, and once, most memorably, Secret – and somehow he gets to be F-dog. Somehow he gets to barely see his kids but still be called a father. Somehow he gets to not do his actual job but still keep his job.

'I feel like I can still hear a buzz,' she says, 'do you think we could –'

'On it,' he snaps, which is what he said last time.

She curses her use of *feel like*. Of *we*. She should just say: Frank, there's a buzz in my headphones, get me new ones. Now she listened, it was more than just a buzz. There's a tapping too. A wire must be loose in there somewhere.

The show is 90s chill, which encompasses everything from late-80s Indigo Girls to early-2000s Scissor Sisters. She makes it as queer as possible, but it just isn't very queer, is it? Queer as in strange, queer as in ruined, queer as in fuck you.

Instead she's playing old songs on BBC Radio, taking calls from LGBTQ people who happen to be awake at 1 a.m. on a week night, sharing their wholesome love stories, celebrating everyone's tolerance and acceptance, raising awareness of ... she's not sure, exactly; carefully avoiding anything sexual or negative or political, keeping it light, keeping it nostalgic. Those *good old days* where she couldn't have married Isa or been the legal parent to the baby Isa is carrying. The show is called Our Pride, because of course it is. In her head she calls it Safe Queers, though she could also have gone with A Lesbian Who Won't Offend Your Gran. A Gay, But Not Like That. She's pretty sure that behind closed doors she's referred to as a triple threat – not because anyone thinks she has three skills, or even one, but because she fits into three neat little boxes: LGBTQ+, regional (which meant the entire UK outside London) and working class (which meant her school didn't have a 'notable alumni' section on Wikipedia, or indeed a Wikipedia page at all). The BBC execs can go tick, tick, tick but only pay one salary.

Sigrid is queer, but not scary queer. She sounds Northern, but of no specific region. She's soon to be a mum, but won't have to take time off with post-partum depression or require a breastfeeding room. Tick, tick, tick. She tells herself that she's playing by their rules but still managing to win the game. Well done her. The Queen of the Queers. A double agent with a flannel shirt and pixie cut. Tick tick tick, goes the sound in her headphones.

'You're on in five,' says Frank, and he doesn't mention the headphones, and neither does she.

'Sounds great, thanks, Frankie,' she says, making sure to keep her voice sweet.

Sigrid wonders if she could get a clothes peg. The smell is unbearable. Isa's the pregnant one; Sigrid can't go around puking. She knows it would look comical, a big wooden peg clipped to her nose, but that might help. Isa can't be offended if it's silly.

Isa's in her third trimester, but her cravings are still at first-trimester intensity. She'll get a desire for something – not even a desire, a need, a *rage* – and want it right this second, and then immediately, sometimes when she hasn't even finished eating it, it becomes repulsive and has to be disposed of. Not even in the kitchen bin; Sigrid has thrown half-eaten plums and bits of pitta bread out in the garden to get them far enough away. A bit of beautifully cooked pork belly suddenly became so awful to Isa that Sigrid had to bury it.

'It's okay that I'm having this, right?' Isa comes up behind Sigrid and slips her arms around her waist, pressing as close as she can, which isn't that close with her bump so big. She's carrying high, which the internet says means a girl. They've had a scan – *Isa* had a scan, Sigrid corrects in her mind; no one scanned Sigrid – but they said they didn't want to know. Sigrid actually does want to know. She wants to know everything. How does it feel to grow someone inside you? A full complement of toenails and a heart and all the tiny bones of the inner ear right in the deepest parts of yourself. She wishes there was a viewing window in Isa's belly so she could see it all. She knows it would be horrifying but she wants to see it anyway. She didn't want to be pregnant, and still doesn't. But she didn't know it would feel like this to be the other mother. She feels so distant.

'Sig? It's okay?' Isa presses closer and Sigrid knows it's not out of affection, but so she can better smell the kidneys frying in the pan. The repulsive, faintly piss-smelling kidneys in their purple-marbled sac. This is love, she thinks. Frying up a pan of pissy organ meat and not puking – that's love.

'Of course it's okay,' she says, tilting her head back so it rests on Isa's shoulder. Her hair is soft and smells of sandalwood. 'It's liver you can't have. Something about vitamin A. But kidneys are a good source of iron. My sister had low iron when she was pregnant.'

'See? My body knows what it needs,' says Isa, sliding her body around Sigrid's, front to front, peppering kisses along her jaw. When they met, Isa had a face full of piercings; so many that people didn't see her face, just the piercings. Sigrid later realised that it was a sign of extreme shyness. Over the years, the piercings disappeared, along with Isa's nerves. Now she's barefaced and brash. Sigrid can still feel a tiny knot of scar under the curve of Isa's lip, catching with each kiss.

At the kitchen table, Sigrid dishes up the kidneys and Isa manages six bites before her expression changes. Sigrid doesn't even wait for her to speak; she whisks the kidneys away, opening all the windows to get rid of the smell. She knows that Isa won't want her to put the kidneys in the bin; she'll say she can still smell them, even through three closed doors and all the way up the stairs. Sigrid takes the dish of kidneys outside. She pauses before locking the back door behind her.

*

The shed is the size of two couches, but it doesn't have any couches in it. It has a shelf made of a rotting scaffolding board, a rusting tin tool-box, a roll of mouldy carpet, a broken plastic slide, a bowl of dusty seashells, a snapped mop.

And the nest.

Isa was the one who first knew about it. She noticed one or two wasps crawling on the cobwebbed window of the shed. Then ten or twelve wasps. Then she realised the wasps weren't on the outside of the glass, but the inside. She dispatched Sigrid to the hardware shop for something to kill the wasps, and hasn't gone within six feet of the shed since. Who knew what those wasp-killing chemicals could do to the baby? Sigrid returned with a plastic-wrapped ball called Wasp Destroyer covered in warning symbols that promised to KILL ALL WASPS DEAD. Surely not all of them, she thinks. If one little thing could kill every wasp, then there wouldn't be any left, and there are absolutely loads of them.

Sigrid stands in the open doorway of the shed. It smells of leaf mould and dust and something else, something she can't name, some-thing almost alien. The wasps' nest is tucked into the back corner of the shed. Papery, heavy, layered with shadow. Hundreds of wasps, small bodies crawling. The scraping sound of them drones, low and metallic. Sigrid feels it in her throat.

She hadn't been able to use the ball of chemicals. The thing about wasps is that they live in any space they can find, spaces that no one else uses or needs. They make a home and a life from what everyone else has discarded. And that's what she and Isa are doing. They'd taken something some man had sold to a fertility clinic without a backward glance, something easily given, something that gets thrown away every day in condoms and tissues and down the toilet – they took it and made something real and true and precious with it. No one wanted Sigrid's radio slot, midnight to 2 a.m., the overnight, the dead hours, the ones no advertisers would buy and no presenters scrambled for, the only one she was offered, the one she immediately took.

She doesn't go any closer in case she accidentally steps on a wasp in the dark. She's read that if a wasp stings or dies, the smell of it makes other wasps swarm. That's why you shouldn't kill a wasp, unless you want its whole family to rally round the corpse of their kin in revenge.

She puts the dish of kidneys on the gritty floor of the shed, then with her foot pushes it closer to the corner. She thinks she hears the buzzing intensify. Can they smell the meat? Do they need the iron? She pushes the dish closer, and this time she's sure the noise changes. She closes her eyes and imagines the feel of the tiny feet on her wrists, her throat, her lips. She imagines the papery mound of the nest against her belly, the rustle and pulse of it as she moves. They're so small. So defenceless. They need a mother.

But they have one, don't they? Somewhere there, in the deepest layer of shadow. Someone, something in there birthed these wasps. Did its body know what it needed? Would it find a way to communicate that to Sigrid? She was doing her best, but it was hard to know what was going on in there. She wishes there was a viewing window in the nest. She feels so distant. She backs out and shuts the door tight.

'I checked the ingredients,' says Frank, handing her a hamper containing fancy chocolates, alcohol-free fizz, something bright pink to put in the bath which looked guaranteed to give you thrush. 'No nuts, so the choccies are safe for Isa to eat.' Sigrid goes to thank him, but then he adds: 'So do you think the baby will call you Dad? It's a great feeling the first time your kid calls you Dad.' And she doesn't know what to say.

What she wants to say is: no, you fucking toolbag, why would the baby call me Dad when I'm not its dad? When I am literally a woman? Is it really so inconceivable that a person can be a mother without a child exiting their body?

She's got her headphones around her neck, and she can hear that they're still buzzing. She opens her mouth to tell him, but he pushes the hamper at her, so what she actually says is: 'Thanks, Frankie. Isa's been craving these.'

That was the problem with Frank: he could be so *nice*. She wanted to put him in a box marked 'homophobe' or 'misogynist', make a complaint about him to HR, even – but how could she when he was giving her thoughtful gifts and enquiring with wide eyes about Isa's morning sickness or whether they'd like Yassine's old pram, it was a good one, they'd barely even used it? All right, he did ask her several times about her husband even after she clearly said the name Isa and the word wife – she'd joked about it with Isa later, like did he think Sigrid meant herself as a wife, but in third person? And all right, she did see him do a little floppy wrist motion when she played Elton John, but perhaps she misunderstood that and he just had a sore wrist.

Her headphones are buzzing louder now. It seems more layered: the buzzing, the ticking, the rustle of small bodies crawling.

If she makes a complaint, she'll be the one labelled difficult. He hadn't even made a joke about lesbians and nuts, even though she's sure he was tempted. That's got to count for something.

'Ayesha told me to tell you she's got recommendations for the best nappies and nipple cream. Speaking of, let me tell you, it's no picnic having to share boobs with a baby. Never thought I'd be jealous of my own son!'

Sigrid smiles and motions at her show notes, a soft head tilt meaning *got to get back to this*. Frank was harmless; just one of those men who don't know how to talk to a queer woman. They either talk to her like they would a straight woman - meaning like a landmine who could explode into inexplicable emotion at any second - or like a man, meaning all blokey nudges and cheeky Nandos and tits. In her mind, she still puts him in the misogynist box, but can't quite bring herself to close the lid.

An hour into the show, the buzzing is so loud she can barely focus. Can't Frank hear it? It's buzzing so loud it's shaking her desk. It's buzzing so loud it's rattling her teeth. She's told Frank so many fucking times about the headphones and still he hasn't changed them, there must be a dozen pairs of fucking headphones in the cupboard and he can't even do that, useless fucking manbaby, can't even change his own child's nappy, doesn't know how to work the dishwasher, asks her what she thinks about the football even though she has zero fucking interest in football but apparently lesbian means man means football, she can see him through the window, he's texting right now, ignoring her even as he's meant to be cueing her in, she has to do half of his job as well as all of her own, she's jumped through every fucking hoop they've put in front of her, even the ones that were on fucking fire, and still, and still this.

The buzzing is in her head, in her wrists and her throat and her lips, the feel of tiny feet, the cloy of decay, of things sprouting, and it comes out, all of it comes out, a swarm of words stinging up out of her.

*

Her boss calls her in. She's never been called in. He doesn't say that Frank made a complaint, but Frank doesn't need to have made a complaint. He's got her recorded, agitated and aggressive. Some of it surely got broadcast before Frank cut to the song.

It's her fault, she knows it's her fault. She should have stayed sweet. Ignored the buzzing. Just sat back and let it happen. Tick, tick, tick. She's valuable because she's Other, but only a little bit. Other-adjacent. Palatable Other. What good is she if they can't fit her into the box?

'Got a beekeeper for you,' says her boss.

It's so far from what she expected him to say that she wonders for a moment if she's having a stroke.

'For me?' she replies, as if receiving a gift, as if he's about to hand her a hamper containing fancy chocolates, alcohol-free fizz and a beekeeper.

'To interview on the show. Reckon it could turn into a six-part piece, if it goes well. Not just the love-story stuff like usual, but the bees. People like bees. And she's trans. He, I mean. So I figured right up your street.'

'But I'm not trans,' says Sigrid.

'You know what I mean. LGBTQLMNOP. Figured you could talk about that.'

About the alphabet? Sigrid wants to say. Instead she says: 'I've got wasps. We can talk about –'

For a moment her boss looks at her with concern. She feels like this might be the first time he's actually looked her fully in the face. 'I said bees, Sigrid, not wasps. Totally different. Wasps don't make anything useful, they're not a functional part of the world. Bees make things and work together. They know their place. Wasps, they're just stinging little bastards that never did anything for anyone.'

She wants the buzzing back. She wants the layered darkness. She wants to be able to sting. She wants to say that she wants new head-phones. She wants to say that she wants a better time slot. She wants to say that she wants Frank and her boss and every straight man, every straight person even, why not, to sink into the ocean.

But she knows that what she needs is honey. She's got nappies to buy. She's got a carrier and a cot and a little plastic baby bath to buy. She's got to cover Isa's half-pay for her mat leave. She can taste the honey in her mouth.

The honey says that she's a good queer. Look, she got her hair cut at a women's salon instead of a barber even though it's three times the cost because apparently a woman's undercut and fade is very different to a man's undercut and fade. Look, she got married, and there were vows and rings and everything. The honey lies thick on her tongue. Look, her wife is pregnant, literally pregnant, and she's a primary-school teacher too, she wears dresses, she gets her bikini line waxed, what more can a lesbian do than that? The honey pools and clogs behind her molars. She doesn't even use the word lesbian in case it offends people. She doesn't use queer in case it offends other people. She doesn't use any word at all. The honey is sealing up in her throat. She can't speak for the sticky thickness of it. She wants to cough it out, but instead she swallows.

'Sounds great, thanks, boss,' she says, and her voice is so sweet.

Isa doesn't want kidneys again, to the extent that even the sight or smell of kidneys, even the memory of kidneys, even the word 'kidney' makes her retch. So Sigrid makes a spag bol. She tells Isa that it's vegan mince, but actually she uses beef instead. She puts only the tiniest dash of red wine in, even though she knows it'll cook off anyway. Isa eats a whole portion, and then a bit more, for the baby. Sigrid understands; she's kept a little of the raw mince aside.

She understands too why you get beekeepers but only wasp destroyers. Everyone's all about bees. Save the bees, feed the bees, buy these specific wildflower seeds to attract bees to your garden. No one wants wasps. They don't make anything, they don't give anything except themselves.

She tells Isa to relax in front of some reality show, and she takes the raw mince out to the shed. She stands in the doorway, feeling the buzz fill out her throat. She's wearing a T-shirt, even though it's cold, so that they can access more skin. The proper name for wasps is *Vespula vulgaris*, and if she could rename her radio show, that's what she'd call it: Vulgar. She's looked up more things about wasps, on her phone in those morning hours which are her night-time, when she should be sleeping, when she should be getting rest now, while she can, before the baby comes. Wasps are sociable and collaborative, working together to build their nests. In the nests grow the wasp larvae. The larvae eat carrion and insects, and the adults feed on the sugary liquid that the larvae secrete. She loves that: the way that they start carnivorous, then consume only the sweetness of their children.

She goes into the shed and pushes the raw mince into the corner, towards the distended paper nest in its layers of shadow. It moves and pulses like a slow-beating heart. There must be thousands of wasps in there. Their bodies crawling over one another in layers, working, building, communing. Vulgar and real.

She feels the buzz in her entire body. The stroke and sting of hungry children on her skin. Her throat feels clear. Not the mawkish, nauseating gloop of honey, but a sharp flake of salt. Something familiar and strange.

She opens the back door.

'Honey?' she calls, and her voice is strong and clear. 'Can you come here? I want to show you something.'

Unbury

Part 1: The Dirt Hole & Its Variations

Avie Thornaby is digging a hole. Beside him the Victrola plays, the vinyl warped, the music woozy. Behind him leans a sign, knocked to a chaotic angle, paint faded so the words LOST LAKE are barely visible. It's dark in the woods. Many small eyes watch him from the trees.

Avie Thornaby is a ferrety man of indeterminate age. He doesn't look young, but there's something unformed about him. He is medium height, skinny, with lank shoulder-length hair and a droopy moustache that he often runs his tongue over. His eyes never stay still. He has one pair of filthy jeans, two work shirts and an infinite number of squashed second-hand hats.

He hears something under the music: a snorting and a hissing.

'Hello?' he calls. From the dark, an owl.

Avie Thornaby leans on his shovel. Fiddles with his cap, leaving dirty finger marks on the brim. Hears nothing but animal sounds, muffled.

The song finishes and the needle catches on a crackling silence. He hears it more clearly now. Not an animal. The sound is elegant and strange, a distant singing, just a whisper above a sigh.

'Who's there?' he calls into the trees. 'This is private property. I will shoot you.'

He doesn't have a gun, and he doesn't own the lake. He lifts a shovel and flips another clod of dirt behind him. That's when he realises. 'The fuck?' he says. The sound is coming from the hole.

He tosses the shovel aside, then thinks better and brandishes it at the hole. 'You come on out now.'

The woods, the night, the Victrola crackle. Even the owl holds its breath.

A white hand bursts from the hole and grabs the earthen side. Another hand emerges and holds tight to Avie's boot.

'You found me,' gasps the woman, using the last of her strength to pull herself out of the hole. 'Thank you. Oh, thank you.'

Avie Thornaby carries the woman through the woods over his shoulders, like a shot steer. She doesn't weigh much. He likes how she smells.

His cabin has smoke coming from the chimney and tarpaper over all the windows. It has YOU HAVE BEEN WARNED painted on it in six-foot-high letters.

In the cabin, his friend Omri Glass is boiling coffee. He looks up when Avie and his burden enter.

'What's this?' he asks, a little surprised, a little envious.

Avie Thornaby deposits the woman on the kitchen chair, where she sits with her hands in her lap, eyes downcast.

'This is my wife,' he says. 'Nola. I'll call you No for short. Do you like that?'

She looks up at him and smiles shyly. 'No.'

'That's right.'

Omri pours coffee thick as treacle and adds sugar. They all drink it together in the half-light of the smoky cabin. There are only two chairs, so Avie stands. After a few sips the sugar hits, and he feels his heart thrash. He rubs his eyes, but the woman doesn't disappear. He takes her cup.

'Come to bed,' he says, and she does.

He wakes in the night. The air feels heavy and there's a pressure on his legs. From another room, he thinks he hears something: a wordless singing, the sound rising and falling. He turns over and goes back to sleep. In the morning, she's in the bed beside him. He reaches out to her and holds one soft, heavy breast in his hand. He squeezes it, testing, though he doesn't know what for.

Part 2: An Expert's Guide to Snaring Methods

Avie Thornaby changes her name to Nora, then Nona. A girl in his school was named something similar. Nona makes runny eggs and coffee for breakfast, potatoes in gravy for dinner, a hot and dark meat stew for supper.

She sings as she cooks, the same tune he heard her sing from the hole, though this time he can hear the words. 'In the ground, in the ground, I was lost and now I'm found. I'll shiver my whole life through.'

He doesn't like the song and tells her to stop. She smiles at him and hums it instead.

He waits until the second night to fuck her. He considers this gentlemanly. He does have to fuck her, though. What else is she there for? A man only needs to eat three times a day and she's here all the time.

The next night he invites Omri Glass for supper and for her. He wants Omri to be envious of his good fortune, but also the men have been through a lot together. Avie knows to share when times are good, so he can get by when times are bad.

The next day, Avie and Omri go out with their traps. She uses the kitchen knife to check her reflection, tilting the scratched blade so it catches the light. She finds a loose edge beneath her left ear and presses it back into place. She lifts her hair and repositions it. It's come in the wrong texture, more like moss, or the silvery fronds of a fern. The sharp brown tips of thorns are beginning to press up beneath her fingernails. She squats over the knife to check between her legs. It's red and swollen, so she squashes the flesh between her fingers a few times to make it stay that way.

She's finished her beauty routine and goes to explore the cabin. In the roof space she finds a chest. She's found such chests before, containing a stolen wolfskin or a sealskin. She opens the chest and paws through it. It's full of long braids of hair: blonde, black, brown, red. Maybe fifteen of them. They're all tied with elastic bands. He could at least have tied them with ribbons, woven in baby's breath or rose petals, made them pretty. The hair smells old.

She starts to wonder: when he dug her up, what was he burying?

Part 3: Adjustment of Leg Hold Traps for Greater Profit

He changes her name to Nova, then forgets and calls her Nola again. It doesn't matter. She makes eggs and lies in his bed.

'No,' she says, smiling, always smiling.

He accuses her of petty treacheries for which she is blameless. He drinks himself into a stupor, cries, then beats her for witnessing it. He tries to trick her into revealing herself. He wakes in the night and hears something from another room.

'In the earth, in the earth, where I waited for my birth. I'll shiver when I come to you.'

There's something wrong with her. He should have known it. What kind of woman would be out there in the woods alone? Not a good one. Not a wife.

'No,' she says, smiling, always smiling.

He makes her open her mouth wide, wider. He checks under her tongue and in the cavities of her cheeks. He lights a match and holds it close to her eyes to watch her pupils change. He holds the soles of her feet to the stove to check that they blister.

He knows there's something. She lies, every night, between heaven and the dirt floor: that endlessly mysterious thing in bed beside him. How can a woman hide something from a man? Why must they always be so secretive, so sneaky? He knows she's a thing from the woods. She can't hide anything from him. He will make her change back.

'Show me,' he demands, then requests, then wheedles. 'Show me what you're hiding.'

'No,' she says.

He can't trust her any more. He needs to sleep, but he has to be safe from her.

There in the wooden chest, gagged, blindfolded, hogtied, she admits defeat. She's tried, but this just isn't working out for her. She thought she'd wanted this life: a plain existence in the woods, a neat little cabin, cooking beans and birthing babies, no underwear and only two dresses so she could wear one while washing the other. A simple trapper's wife, with only trapper's wife problems. Even a poacher or bootlegger had a certain purity. As easy as falling off a log. As easy as pie.

She shakes off her bonds and opens the chest.

She stands by the bed, looking down at Avie Thornaby. There are so many things she could have been. She's screamed war cries from the prow of her husband's fleet. She's poisoned her husband's entire dynasty. She's been draped in perfumed furs and gleamed like a trophy at her doomed husband's side. She's been splashed in blood from her husband's assassination. She can be all of it, everything, and all she needs is a man with a little imagination.

And what did this man choose? A hole.

Poor Avie Thornaby, who dug up a woman and never asked who buried her.

Part 4: Evaluation of Lures, Baits & Urines

In the cabin, Avie Thornaby and Omri Glass and three other men whose names she never heard are laid out in a line, side by side. They are naked. There are very few marks on their bodies. They lie on their backs, mouths and eyes wide open, hungry for nothing, peeping up the skirts of nothing. She's eaten the parts she likes and leaves the rest for the other animals.

No, they'd all said as their final word. She quite likes that name and might keep it for next time. It feels lucky, the fact that they all remembered her name right to the end.

It's easy to feel fond of them like this. Helpless and kind of silly. Their little dicks flopped to the side like worms. Their tobacco-stained teeth, cavities visible. Avie's and Omri's hands are almost touching. Did they ever touch in life? When they both put their little dicks in her, did their eyes meet over her shoulder? Did they smell one another's sweat and semen? Was that the whole point of it?

She drinks off the water butt to the last drop, the rainfall cold and sweet. She can still taste them a little, but it will pass. She takes the shovel and nothing else.

She'll try the other side of the lake. She doesn't want to get too close to the water; last time she ended up with a fish hook snagged in the roof of her mouth. She didn't like having salt crusted around her eyes, or wrinkled fingertips.

This side of the lake is closer to the city. The earth here is harder and lighter, and most of the prey animals have been spooked off. It might be a while until someone comes by. But she knows there are subterranean wells, and there might be scouts for new housing developments. Someone always comes eventually.

She digs a hole, then squats beside it. She urinates into the rich earth, then takes some leaves and wipes around her vagina. She could buy a scent spray with the correct pheromones, but she prefers to do it this way. Since she's fed, from the divot in her lower back she's sprouted a peacock tail of ferns which she can open and close at will. It's a shame to lose that, but we're all born naked.

She slides into the hole and pulls at the earth, letting it collapse onto her. The soil is the colour of biscuit crumbs, studded with seeds, tasting of woodlice and malt. She breathes it in, letting it fill her. Her eyes close and she lets herself sleep.

She waits to transform; waits to see who will unbury her.

Darling

Darling[1], Season 10[2] Episode[3] 3_

FADE IN:

1 INT. BROWNSTONE - BATHROOM - NIGHT.[4]

---

1 You're reading my notes on this script because you're a fan of the genre. Whatever the hell this genre is. Copaganda. Crime of the week. Empowered feminist detective. Opportunity for looky-loos to coo and sleaze over crying women.

2 We ran for a full 13 seasons. That's a lot of looky-loos.

3 A lot of crying women.

4 Did you cry too? Watching me, did you cry? I bet you did. I was good. At my best, I was so damn good.

A swanky[5], modern[6] bathroom[7]. Expensive fittings and, in the middle, a waterfall shower with translucent glass panels. Faint music drifts in from the next room.

The only discordant note is a trail of clothes across the floor, abandoned as their owner made her way to the shower. The water is on, and we see the shapely silhouette of a young woman[8] showering.

                SHOWERING WOMAN (O.S.)

---

5   My husband cried, watching me. When I was almost raped in prison, going under-
    cover to entice a confession from a serial killer. He cried for his fear for what could
    happen to me – or to Darling, I guess. He said that watching that scene, he knew he
    had to have me.

6   And six months later we were married. Turns out you can get everything you want. If
    what you want is a washed-up but still-hot TV actress now making no-budget shit-
    shows in the middle of nowhere.

7   I wasn't there for this scene. Just telling you that right now. It was someone younger.
    Blonder. Not that I care. Dumb bitch. She'll see soon enough. Needs to get some rape
    scenes under her belt first. Well, *Darling* will help with that.

8   *Darling* was about me from the start. The whole goddamn damn show was written
    around me. Maybe not the pilot, but for sure the rest. The others – Flintlock, even
    Sweets – they came in later. I'd seen 2Cool in a movie before he was brought in as
    Flintlock, but like most people I knew him from rap. He'd like us to forget about that.
    Every season they try to write it into the show, give him a reason to have to rap some-
    thing, going undercover at a hip-hop club or some goddamn thing, but he always
    vetoes. It's cheesy, and even that cheesy bastard 2Cool knows it.

DARLING

(sings[9])

Oh girl, oh girl, don't you lie to
me. Where did you sleep last night?

Camera pushes in through a gap in the glass panels.
We see the back[10] of the woman[11] as she faces[12] the

---

9 His name isn't really 2Cool. No parent would be so cruel. It's Ronald. But every day on set I called him 2Cool, just because I could. Got to remind these guys of their place, or they'll try to take yours.

10 I did a bunch of these roles when I was starting out. Cry 'n' dies. You spend most of the time crying and running from the killer, and then you die – in your underwear, or a bathing suit, if the director can find a reason. Mostly in horror movies but you do get them in crime shows like this. The ones I did were in horror. I've been murdered by so many men. Tortured, too. Raped, both on-screen and off-, the camera cutting away just as he rips off my pantyhose. It's always pantyhose, if you're wondering. Must be some fetish thing. I live in seasonless LA, when the hell would I ever need to wear pantyhose?

11 I didn't mind those roles. At least they paid, and they were fast. You could get them done in a day, easy. And there wasn't hours in the makeup chair, like for those SFX movies. Just a lot of lying around covered in sugar syrup with dead leaves stuck to you. The main thing is if it was shot outside there'd be flies on your face, but you couldn't move, not even to blow them away, because of continuity. For the crying part, fake tears were optional. I never needed them. Plenty to cry about, I'd say, but jokey, because what would a beautiful 19-year-old ever have to cry about?

12 I guess it makes sense to me, the cry 'n' die. Circle of life. At the start, we cry. At the end, we die. Maybe I'll cry at the end too, who knows?

spraying[13] water[14], lathering her long[15] blonde hair. On her shoulder is a delicate rose tattoo.

SHOWERING WOMAN (CONT'D)

In the pines, in the pines, where the sun never shines, I shivered the whole night[16] long.

---

13 My mother didn't cry at the end. I know that. There wasn't time for anything. Sometimes I imagine it – I don't want to imagine it, but that's the curse of having a fast brain, it goes against me sometimes – and then I hear her at the end. She tries to say my name, Chastity, she says, Chastity, barely audible through her bubbling mouthful of blood, and she reaches for me, reaches out for her baby where I'm bawling and grabbing for her from the back seat, and our hands touch, our fingertips grasp, and she looks me right in the eye with such love, with such intense devotion and fierce tenderness, and then she dies and I carry that look with me for the rest of my life like a talisman.

14 That's just the sweetest bullshit, baby, as my husband would say. You know it is. Everyone knows the story of how my mother died and I'm not going to tell a different version, in particular not here, scrawled on a lazy-ass knock-em-out conveyor-belt script. She was decapitated, dead instantly, no words and no bubbling blood and no reaching. And I went from asleep to unconscious and I never even knew anything about it until I woke up in the ER, washed clean and with my brothers lying one on either side, all of us wearing someone else's clothes.

15 There's a whole website for it. Dead Actresses. Imaginative name, right? I guess no one wants to see dead actors. I'm on it too. Stills of all my death scenes. Or most of them. My mother's, too. Not the real one. Only the movie ones.

16 I wonder if my death scene from this movie will be there too.

Through the glass[17] panel, we see[18] a silhouette[19] of
a man[20] approaching[21].

SHOWERING WOMAN (CONT'D)
Oh girl[22], oh[23] girl, where[24] did
you go[25]?

---

17 People are more interested in the story of my mother's death than any story I've
acted.

18 I've told the story so many times. My publicist says I won't discuss it but I always do.
I probably wouldn't get on the talk shows at all without that story. Plus I spent a long
time perfecting the single, gleaming tear at the crucial moment.

19 I don't remember anything. I don't remember her. I've told the story so many times I
don't even know if it's true. My husband used to get me to tell it to him over and over
and over. Therapy, he said, to heal me.

20 I don't think it healed me. Not one damn goddamn bit.

21 I could get on the shows without the story back when I was Darling. But now I'm not
Darling. I'm Chastity Charles.

22 I used to have a different name, did you know that? My mother changed it when I was
a week old. Said the other name didn't suit me. I don't even know what that other
name was.

23 I became Chastity the way I became Darling. I'm good at that.

24 It's a kind of method acting, don't you think?

25 You never hear stories about actresses doing method. Actors, sure; not showering for
months or mailing dead rats to their co-stars. Actresses would be fired instantly. Or
maybe they don't need it. Women don't need to play games. We know how to just *act*.

The man cocks[26] his head[27] to watch the woman, then slips his hand through the doors and caresses her lower back. The camera follows his hand and we see his wedding ring.

             SHOWERING WOMAN (CONT'D)
                (smiling now)
        You're going where the cold –

She turns and sees the man. For a moment she looks surprised, then covers it. She shuts off the shower.

---

26 chastity (noun): the state or practice of refraining from extramarital, or from all, sexual intercourse.

27 My mother looked at her week-old baby, and the best name she could think of meant not having sex. I don't know what else to say about that.

34

DARLING

SHOWERING WOMAN

You're home[28] early[29], baby[30]. Hand me
a towel?

He doesn't.

                    MAN

Didn't know it was me, huh, baby?

                   WOMAN

Oh, silly. Of course I knew it was
you. Who else would it be? Now come
on, I'm getting cold.

---

28 I wonder what kind of room you're picturing imagining me in. I know you're imagining picturing me. You know exactly what Chastity Charles looks like. Fade in: night. A
dump of a motel room with a view of a chain-link fence and an audience of some kind
of scrub weed. It's in the middle of some godforsaken goddamn desert and it's day
five of a twelve-day shoot. What the goddamn can you shoot in only twelve days? I
hear you ask. The answer is an entire picture, all ninety useless minutes of it, though
the slug's pace we're going I doubt we'll get half done. *Desert Rats III*. That's how they
wrote it on the script. Not three. Aye-aye-aye.

29 The sun is going down. Sky burning red. A hideous hour.

30 Would be good to say I was sipping from an airplane vodka bottle, wouldn't it? My
coat pockets clinking with them. Drinking them straight to save on calories and to get
shitfaced faster. Heard about a guy once, a real boozer, fucked up his life, wife left him,
all that. And his poison was Babycham. Babycham! Not whiskey, not beer, not even
wine. Goddamned embarrassing is what that is.

                    MAN
        You're gonna know all about cold.
        Baby.

He approaches her menacingly. Camera pulls out,
tracking out of the bathroom. We hear the woman
scream.

                              FADE OUT.

            END OF TEASER

ACT ONE[31]

FADE IN:

2 INT. FLINTLOCK'S OFFICE - DAY.

The office is cluttered and dingy. Darling enters,
holding a takeout coffee.

                  DARLING
        You wanted me, chief[32]?

---

31 I don't know why I brought this *Darling* script. I'm only meant to sign it so it can go on
   some memorabilia website. Big scrawl, *Chastity Charles xxx*, with a heart over the 'i'. A
   memento. Something to remember me by.

32 My husband's idea. He's always looking out for me. He knows what people want of
   me. Of Chastity, I mean. When the paychecks shrink, there's still money to be made on

DARLING

FLINTLOCK

Thought you were off the caffeine.

DARLING

It's herbal tea. That's what you
wanted[33] me for[34]?

---

the con circuit, memorabilia, all that shit. Your shine might fade but that doesn't mean you have to actually *die*, you know?

33 Funny thing about this movie. I knew it was gonna be low budget but it is *low god-damned budget*. Skeleton crew doesn't even cover it. I'm doing my own hair and makeup. Wardrobe is just what I was wearing when I arrived – and what was under it. The screenwriter, director, DP, producer and, I think, editor are all the same guy. There's only one other actor, and he's playing my lover-slash-killer. I don't know if I'm the desert rat (aye-aye-aye) or he is.

34 My mother came out swinging, career-wise. Some early glamour shots, couple of big studio pictures playing the pretty dumb blonde, marry a ball player, pop out three kids, tragic death. But she did work in those in-between years, the low times between the big pictures and the kids. Bet you didn't know that. Not many people do. A few horror pictures, some porn. Not like we'd think of it now. Not nasty stuff. Left a lot more to the imagination back then. 'Nudey pictures', she'd have called them. I've seen them. Not the nudey pictures. The horrors. In one of them she was pregnant with me. Her bump was small and she did her best to hide it, but you can see it if you know when to look.

FLINTLOCK

Darling[35], how long have we[36] been
together[37]?

DARLING

You mean . . . ?

FLINTLOCK

On the beat. Catching perps. Getting
justice for dead girls[38].

---

35 My first screen role.

36 I overheard my mother talking to a girlfriend once. She said that when she told the
    director she was pregnant with me, he told her to have an abortion. She simply
    replied: no.

37 They really tried to make this work, Darling and Flintlock. That Sam/Diane, Mulder/
    Scully, will they/won't they tension. Didn't work. Because I didn't want it to goddamn
    work. The guy was bald! He had hair on the backs of his hands, hair poking up out of
    his shirt collar, hair in his asscrack I bet, but on his head? Nada. I swear, every guy
    they set me – set Darling – up with in the whole 13-season run was beneath her. It's
    not just me saying that. It was *Entertainment Weekly*. They did a whole list, 'Disap-
    pointing Couples of Primetime', and we were number goddamned 6.

38 What kind of real cop would say that? 'Dead girls'? It's unprofessional. But 'female
    victim' doesn't work on TV. It's not titillating. It's cold. Clinical. You feel sorry for a
    female victim. But dead girls, you can still fuck.

She takes[39] a seat[40]. Flips open a file[41] on the desk,
closes it again.

                    DARLING
         Almost two years.

                    FLINTLOCK
         You ever regret coming here?

                    DARLING
         Didn't have much choice, chief.
              (sighs)
         I'm here because I want to be.
         Trying to have a real life for a
         change. You?

---

39 What kind of real cop ever gave a shit about a dead girl anyway? NHI: no humans
   involved. That's what they say about the whores and junkies. I know because they
   sent us on ride-alongs to get a feel for the vibes, the voice, the body language. NHI, I
   heard them say, every single night.

40 That's why *Darling* mattered. No NHIs on our show. We gave a voice to the voiceless.

41 I'd trot out that line in interviews. Back when I used to get interviewed. Tight forehead and tight dress on some Friday-night show. We made it seem like we were
   setting the cops to rights, but far from it. The whole show was cop propaganda, I see
   that. Important to make a distinction between a bad cop (doesn't give a shit about a
   dead whore) and a good cop (catching perps and getting justice for dead girls). Bad
   cops are just bad apples. Funny how we'd always forget the rest of that phrase.

39

FLINTLOCK

I've had my fill of real life.
Speaking of which, there's movement
on the Emily Irons case.

He hands her a file. Emily's photo inside.

FLINTLOCK (CONT'D)

We got a guy looks good for it.
Worked out of the same building as
Emily. Witnesses say his attention[42]
to her was, and I quote,
'inappropriate[43]'. Which I[44] guess
means he was a creep[45].

DARLING

We bringing him in?

---

42 Forgot what I was saying there. The motel-room phone just rang. My husband. He's so sweet. Always checking on me.

43 This room, this movie. It's getting to me. I swear I could hear my own voice in the background on the call. I asked my husband and he didn't laugh it off and he didn't deny it. Just asked me in a concerned voice if I was alone, if I was okay.

44 Another funny thing about this movie. The location. I know I said motel but I don't even think this is a motel any more. It feels abandoned. I think we're just here for the movie. But the director didn't say anything about filming in this room. I should have a trailer, don't you think? A girl like me? Don't I deserve that?

45 'Are you all alone?' my husband says. Of course I'm not alone, you sweet, soft idiot. I'm never really alone. I have all of you.

DARLING

FLINTLOCK

We got no reason to. We need a
way in.

DARLING

You mean you need a honeytrap[46].[47]

FLINTLOCK[48]

You're[49] a good[50] undercover.

DARLING

That was before I was made[51]. Between
the shooting and the Mack Culverin

---

46 Spoiler! The honeytrap did not go to plan. There was a rape. I was raped. When we
were filming that scene I told myself it was a useful thing to do. It was good, to show
people that even the great Meredith Darling, even the great Chastity Charles, could be
a victim, could be –

47 Let me try that again. While on a case, Darling was set upon by a gang of men. She was
wearing a wire but it malfunctioned. One of the other cops was crooked, he set it up,
but that won't come out until later in the season. For now it's just her and a gang of
men and a dimly lit room and –

48 It was the way they were all watching it back. The whole crew. All men. It's always all
men. Watching it back on the monitors, my screams repeating, rewind and repeat,
screaming forever, the reflections, my face reflecting in their eyes as they watched.

49 My tits. My tears.

50 My husband never watches me. I like that about him. He's not in the industry.

51 My husband is precious to me. He's not like other men.

thing, everyone knows now that I
work[52] for the justice[53] department.

FLINTLOCK
And everyone knows the department
turned on you.

Darling sips her tea and thinks[54].

DARLING
So I'm[55] the disgraced[56] cop looking
for revenge? That's a role I can
play[57].

---

52 He did watch that one scene though. I know because he said it made him cry. But he doesn't watch me any more, not now he's got the real thing.

53 That scene. When he called, that's the voice I heard in the background. Darling, shirt unfastened, white lace bra, getting fitted for the wire.

54 Funny thing about this hotel. I've been here before, thirty years ago. My mother filmed a picture here. The horror one. The one that I'm in too, inside her.

55 Such a strange coincidence.

56 You know what's a pisser? A real goddamned pisser? I could play any role. I really could. Given half a chance I could have been Meryl goddamn Streep.

57 And what did I get? A bunch of cry 'n' dies, my prime years swallowed up by 13 seasons of Meredith goddamned Darling, and now some bare-bones barrel-scraping on *Desert Rats* aye-aye-aye.

DARLING

> FLINTLOCK
> Might be a way back in for you,
> Darling[58]. I know you miss[59]
> undercover.

> DARLING
> You have no idea what I miss[60].

She looks again at Emily's photo, then stands up.

> DARLING (CONT'D)
> I'll do it.

CUT TO:

3 INT. DARLING'S APT - NIGHT.

The apartment is classy, but cardboard boxes stuffed with files are stacked under the coffee table. Darling and Sweets are still in their work clothes, but rumpled now.

---

58 My husband gets it. He's always known what's best for me. He chose this movie for me and there must be a reason. I have to keep trusting him.

59 I don't miss her. I don't. What's to miss? I barely knew her.

60 Why is he watching that episode? What is he looking for?

Sweets refills[61] both their glasses.

DARLING

I've spent ten years pushing rape
victims to testify — telling them
they're so brave to come forward,
it's not their fault, they're
strong . . . But until you go through
it yourself . . .

SWEETS

You want me to tell you it's not
your fault[62]? Cos I think[63] —

---

61 My husband encouraged me to go for this picture. He's always been so supportive. I
didn't even read the script, I hated the title so much. But he read it – stayed up late
reading it over and over. Scrawled on it, suggestions for how I could play lines, how
the camera could come close to my face, how loud to scream, the best point to cry.

62 That wasn't true about the tiny vodka bottles. I haven't touched a drop. I want you to
remember that when I tell you that someone is peeping in my windows. I've checked
and I've called down to the desk and there's no one there. But there is someone there.

63 They tap-tap-tippity-fucking-tap on the window. Then when I yank the drapes back
they're gone. The drapes, probably some shade called cocoa brown, chocolate dream,
hazelnut ecstasy, but let's be real, it's the shade of a red-wine shit, and the fabric is
greasy, probably from where some reprobate jacked off onto them. They're watching.
Some long-lens fucker is trying to get a shot. I know it.

DARLING

(coughs, hard, covers[64] by sipping her wine)

\- I think you already know.

DARLING

It's over now.

SWEETS

So you're doing this for what - for
closure? Revenge? A second chance?

DARLING

(guard down)

There are some things, you can put
them behind you, but they do change
you. I just wish I could do
something about the nightmares . . .

SWEETS

Nightmares[65]? About Mack Culverin?

---

64 My first kiss was on camera. My first date. My first wedding. I played it all for roles
before I played it for real. When I married my husband, it felt practised. Inevitable. I
kept waiting for someone to yell *cut*.

65 I've turned the TV on to block the noise from outside. I can't flip the channel, can't
find the goddamn remote. It's her. And it's me. On the screen, there, tiny, inside her. Of
course they'd be showing this movie. Of course it would be this night in this place.

Darling notices[66] Sweets[67] reaching[68] for her voice[69] recorder, touches[70] her[71] hand[72].

DARLING

Can we keep[73] that particular nightmare off the record?

SWEETS

Technically you're meant to say off the record first, but —

---

66 Funny thing about this movie, part three. Part aye-aye-aye. I signed an NDA. Not unheard of, but for something like this . . .

67 I mean who gives a good goddamn about *Desert Rats III*? The director has been so secretive. Told me not to tell anyone I was in the movie. Not to tell anyone where I was going. To leave my cell phone and credit cards at home. Picked me up in a rental car so I didn't have to bring my own. He hasn't let me read a full script or know the movie's ending. Says it'll all become clear when the time is right. Thinks he's some kind of creative genius, probably. They all do.

68 So if no one knows I'm here, then how did the photographers find me?

69 This is all getting to me. I'm seeing things. I swear I saw the face of the photographer as the camera flashed, and it was my husband.

70 The TV screen. The big black window behind it.

71 I see her on the screen. I see me reflected behind her.

72 I see me, inside the TV, inside her.

73 My husband isn't here. He can't be here.

DARLING

(puts the recorder back in her purse)
— I don't want to give any of those
pricks the satisfaction.

DARLING

I thought when I called, the wine
and the hour would suggest 'off the
record'[74].

SWEETS

Since when did a late night[75] or a
bit of booze switch off a cop's
instinct?

Darling sips her wine, then settles back on the
couch, edging closer to Sweets. Sweets shuffles
closer[76] too.

SWEETS

So why did you call[77] me?

---

74 He's at home, watching me be raped.

75 He played that scene back, over and over. I know he did. Some nights he thought I'd
taken my sleeping pill but I flushed it instead. From downstairs I could hear Darling
scream. My own desperate cries. My tears.

76 The phone is ringing. I know it's him. I know I have to answer. But I can't bear to hear
myself.

77 He doesn't need me, not now. I don't even look like her any more.

47

As Darling's[78] phone vibrates, she pulls it out[79] —

SWEETS (CONT'D)

TO be continued[80].

FADE OUT.

END OF ACT[81] ONE

---

78 No one wants me. They never did. They only ever wanted her.

79 Here's the thing about Meredith Darling. It's the same as the thing about Chastity Charles. I'm not her. I don't know who I am, what my real name is, and I never will. Maybe it doesn't even matter. The best of me is the part that was recorded. Chastity, Meredith. That other girl – no one ever wanted to film her.

80 I wonder if I'll cry at the end, in the scene where my lover kills me.

81 It doesn't matter now what happens to me, because he has the best of me. He has Darling. He has the show, forever. The tits, darling, the tears. You'll always have that.

Wreckage

olly lies, staring up at the ceiling. The lights from the Ferris wheel strobe across her face: now red, now pink, now green. She wonders if the colours are highlighting her wrinkles, or smoothing them out in a flattering glow. She realises she doesn't care. She also realises that Albie is pumping in time with the changing colours. Red – pump. Pink – pump. Green –

He slips a pillow over her face, and she's glad: because the smell of frying doughnuts is making her feel hungry and sick at the same time, and because that means he's nearly finished. He presses the pillow down and all she can hear is her own heartbeat, that low, slow boom. She holds her breath and lets the hot red throb fill her ears. He thrusts a final time, shudders, and removes the pillow.

'All done, love,' he says, unnecessarily. Molly smiles; reaches out and pats whichever of Albie's body parts is making that lump in the duvet. She used to love his body parts, she really did. He recently read in a *Good Housekeeping* article in the GP's office that vaginal dryness is common for women in their fifties. Molly is forty-nine but she let him buy the lube anyway.

She opens her eyes. She can smell doughnuts. She's hungry and sick. Aroused and repulsed. Complacent and furious. She watches the lights strobe across the ceiling; hears the clatter of the roller coaster, the blaring hurdy-gurdy tune, the recorded cackle of the ghost-train skeleton.

She tunes it out. Under it all, somewhere in the depths, is the sound of the sea. The waves shush in and out, in and out. A languid slow-fuck, a wish made real.

Molly wakes in silence and black. For a second she thinks Albie has put the pillow over her face again. But she reaches out and the air before her is clear and cold. She feels her way to the window and pulls back the curtain. Pale orange velvet, like fondant inside cheap choco-lates. The fabric feels damp in the January chill and she crosses her arms, tucking her hands under her breasts to warm them.

There must be a power cut. No lights, no sounds but for the stars and the sea. She doesn't know how she and Albie both slept through the storm; it must have been a big one to knock out the whole town's power. The rain has stopped now. The wind, the hail, the thunder and fuss and noise.

Outside their bedroom window is the high street, then the dark-ened carnival, then a strip of sand, then the restless sea. All is still in the winter dark. Everything is covered in a sheen of ice, as if it's been sugar-glazed. The mechanical arms of the carnival rides look like the bleached skeletons of long-dead monsters. Even the litter on the high street is frosted white like bonbons.

Molly slides her hands from her breasts to press against her belly. Albie called her stretch marks *silverfish*, back when he used to look at her and she used to like him looking. And he was right, they did shine silver, the tiny indents where something grew in her before the rest of her was ready.

Clouds uncover the moon and suddenly Molly sees: beyond the carnival, the beach is covered in starfish. Hundreds, hundreds of starfish. Frozen solid, they shimmer like fallen stars.

Then she sees something else.

A woman.

In the moonlight she gleams silver, brighter than every bulb at the carnival. She picks her way across the beach, draped in what looks like a length of starlight, and goes into one of the empty caravans by the rocks. The caravan door clicks shut and the moon is covered again. Molly keeps watching, but the show is over.

Nothing in the restaurant ever changes. Nothing in the restaurant has changed since Albie's mother Albina died ten years ago. The red tablecloths and garish leather booths, the CD of tarantella songs, the tackety suck of each step on the chequerboard lino floor.

Each table holds, of course, a candle in an old wine bottle layered in melted wax. The candles provide little light; they're for ambiance, and so that Molly can burn her elbows as she passes plates; the coloured lights from the carnival outside make the restaurant dazzlingly bright. The power was out for a full day after the storm. The local newspaper columnist called it, rather grandly in Molly's opinion, 'The Night of a Thousand Stars'.

The starfish are still there a week later. They're still frozen, but when the thaw comes they'll start to rot. No one wants to walk on them and the beach is deserted. Molly assumes the council will come and remove them at some point. She wonders if they'll be swept back into the sea, or chucked into a bin lorry. If it'll be the black bins for landfill or the brown bins for organic waste. A thousand frozen starfish in a municipal compost bin.

NO & OTHER LOVE STORIES

'Can I interest you in any of our specials?' she asks a couple on a date. The man's hair looks like it's been fried in batter. The woman's red patent heels are plump and greasy like lipstick. 'We do a discount for true love,' Molly says, and the couple light up.

'Italy is for lovers!' calls out Albie in his strongest accent as he passes, wielding two plates piled high with meatballs. Molly isn't sure if it's offensive, the accent, but she's not Italian and Albie is, so she can't really say anything. Everyone wants a story, and he's trying to give them one. The couple order a special.

The restaurant should be called Mezzasalma's, for Albie Mezzasalma. But 'Mezzasalma' translates as 'half dead'. As in deadbeat. As in dullard. Molly has never made comment about this, not even jokingly, and she doubts that any actual Italian speakers come in here anyway, but Albie's mother Albina called it Mezza when she opened it, which is what it's always been called and what it always will be called.

If Molly were to name a restaurant in this town, she'd call it the Home Scar. It's the mark that limpets leave when they cling to a rock. The longer the limpet sticks in the same place, the deeper the scar and the safer the limpet.

'This restaurant,' she says to a family of six, smiling, as she's piling up their sauce-smeared dishes, 'used to be called the Home Scar. We renamed it Mezzasalma's when a mermaid came up out of the sea one day.' Everyone wants a story, she knows. Albie once called her a compulsive liar, and she called him a hypocrite. The family all have wispy blonde hair, and the lights from outside dye it harlequin colours. 'Because mezza means half, and the mermaid was half –'

There is someone on the beach. Someone beyond the roller-coaster screams and garish lights. Someone treading lightly across the backs of the frozen stars. It's the woman from the night of the storm. Even from this distance, even in the dark, even in glimpses in the slow-strobing space left as the Ferris wheel turns, Molly is sure. Perhaps not a woman, but a teenage girl. She shimmers in the winter evening, translucent, colourless. The only thing not dyed bright by the carnival. She seems to exist behind it, beneath it. A thing from the deep sea.

'Are you half?' says one of the children, or at least that's what Molly hears. She smiles vaguely and fetches the dessert menu.

The candy-bright lights. The candy-bright drinks. The candy-bright dresses on Molly and Trish and Dorota and Mia and Cathryn and Liz and Heather. All of the village wives, sucked in and pouted out, cheersing their glasses around a nightclub table at 2 a.m.

Molly's shoes feel too tight and she wonders if her feet can have grown. Do feet do that, keep growing? She knows that ears and noses do; that's why old people, old men in particular, always seem to have huge ears, like elephants.

'Do you ever think your husband looks like an elephant?' she yells to Liz under the pounding music, and Liz smiles around her straw and closes her eyes and sways happily to the beat. Molly doesn't know if Liz actually heard her. Probably not. The music is so loud she can feel it in her throat. It feels like that time she suggested to Albie that he might like to choke her during sex. He didn't like it, and never did it again. Molly doesn't know if she liked it; he didn't do it long enough for her to pass out, which was what she really wanted.

'I rode an elephant once,' Molly yells in Liz's ear. 'I was travelling in India and I had this boyfriend, not really a boyfriend actually, more like a maharajah who had taken a shine to me. He said I was worth fifty elephants. I don't know if that's a lot but it sounds like a lot, doesn't it?'

'Yeah, yeah!' says Liz, her voice a press on Molly's eardrums. She puts down her drink and tugs Molly to the smoking area. The door shuts behind them and the sudden drop in noise feels like a loss, a hollowing.

'I don't think he looks like an elephant,' says Liz, accepting a lit cigarette from a man young enough to be her nephew's boyfriend. 'I think he looks like a fish. One of those deep-sea kinds with a light on their head. Every morning he opens the curtains and then just stands there blinking, like daylight is a surprise.'

Molly thinks of Liz's husband. He's got a name that sounds like a euphemism for a penis, Willy or Billy or Tony. She can never remember husbands' names. He comes to Albie's backyard poker games every fortnight. His glasses make his eyes look tiny, and now she thinks about it, he does blink a lot.

'I can see that,' she says. Liz tips the cigarette towards her. She accepts it, then wishes she hadn't, and gives it back without inhaling. Then she wishes she had it, just for something to hold, but it's too late.

'I just want some space in the bed,' says Liz to the cigarette. No, not to the cigarette: to the light glowing at the tip of it, to the thin stream of pale smoke. 'His feet are freezing and his toenails scratch.'

'I could knit him some socks,' says Molly. 'If that would –'

'Have you noticed Mia is looking really well?' interrupts Liz. 'She says she fancies rock climbing. She was into it before she got married. Do you ever think about that?'

'Rock climbing?'

'About what you could be without him.' Liz takes a drag with an air of finality. 'You don't have to feel bad for wanting more, Moll.' Liz flips her cigarette against the wall and watches the sparks.

*

The greenhouse is opaque with smoke. It coils and distorts, white on white, and Molly thinks of a length of starlight. Standing at the open back door, nipples hardening and nose starting to run in the cold air, all she can see through the greenhouse glass is eight feet: leather loafers, tatty trainers, canvas slip-ons and, optimistically for the weather, a pair of Velcro-strapped walking sandals. Someone shifts, waving an arm, and the smoke clears for a moment. Albie brays a laugh, eyes closing.

There is nothing green in the greenhouse. There is cigar smoke, and a floor of wobbly paving slabs, and some folding plastic chairs, and an old sawhorse as a table, and a pack of cards, and Albie's boys. Except they're not boys, of course, they're fiftysomething men with hairy knuckles and sagging testicles. Still –

'Boys!' is what Molly says, pushing open the greenhouse door with her Lycra-clad hip. 'Boys, here's your snacks,' and she almost wants – can she really, actually want? – one of them to make a pass, grab her arse, say something, *wink* even, behind Albie's back. Her dress is tight and red and surely that's enough. She told one of the boys once that she'd met Albie when she was working in a strip club; that he'd saved her. She'd told another that her parents were rich but negligent, that she'd renounced her inheritance and run away with her Biology teacher from her international school in Brussels. She'd told another that she'd grown up in a cult, though of course she didn't call it that; just said her family had been 'religious, but the bad kind' and left the rest to his imagination. She'd even winced a little and raised her hand to her chest, wondering if he'd imagine some kind of whipping or pricking of thorns. Men liked saving women. She tried to be a woman who needed saving.

They're just a group of tired, quiet men playing cards on a Tuesday night and she's not sure she actually wants any of them. But she could. She should.

The boys don't wink. They take the dishes of honey-roast peanuts and pickled lupini and nod politely at her. She almost expects them to call her Mrs Mezzasalma, and then she'd have to make a joke about how that's her mother-in-law, and then she'd have to make sure Albie didn't see her shudder at the thought of being connected to Albina. But they don't say anything, and Albie takes her hand and kisses the back of it, absent-minded and gallant, tender and unthinking, without raising his gaze from his cards, and she squeezes his hand and leaves, and she wants to love him again. She wants to want to. But she can't stop thinking about what Liz said. What could she be without him? What could they all be?

On her third date with Albie, she told him that she'd had a baby as a teenager and given it up for adoption. She'd planned to call it Stella if it was a girl. For a boy, Sol. But when the baby came out of her, they took it away, and she didn't know if it was a girl or a boy, and she didn't call it anything at all.

Albie held her hand between the salt and pepper shakers, looking into her eyes and not speaking. When they slept together, he always took care to kiss her belly, but never to linger.

Another version of the story is that she did see the baby, because it had to be six weeks old before it could be adopted. But she didn't want to wait six weeks. She couldn't. She turned her face to the window and said that if she was left alone with the baby then she would not feed it or clean it or look at it. She didn't say she would kill it, or even that she would let it die, but that is what she meant. That's why they took the baby away.

She thinks this happened. She's told both versions of the story, so either one could be true.

'Reckon he's off with her from the takeaway,' says a voice from the greenhouse.

'He'd be so lucky,' says another. 'Daft sod's asleep in his car somewhere.'

'Bet he's gone to see his sister over east.'

'Without telling Mia?'

No reply, just the slap of cards on the table.

Molly hadn't realised one of the boys was missing.

But now she thinks about it, there are usually ten feet under the smoke.

Molly waits until Albie is asleep before slipping out. She doesn't need to keep this from him, but there's a thrill in having a secret. She shrugs on her green faux-fur coat and tips the collar up around her face, but still the wind numbs her cheeks and pulls tears from her eyes.

It's 4 a.m. and the street is empty. Even the drunken stragglers from the 80s-revival nightclub have staggered home. Even the seagulls have had their fill of chips. Even the carnival sleeps. It's just her and the starfish.

She thought they'd crunch under her feet, the way old bones do when they've been brought in by the tide. But instead they clatter like blocks of glass. She doesn't know why everyone was so unwilling to walk on them; it's like stepping on a glass path, right to the sea. Night of a Thousand Stars. It doesn't seem so grand now.

She follows the starfish to where the sea starts. She stands on a pile of glazed bodies, feeling the chill through the soles of her Uggs.

A light blinks on at the corner of her eye. Not the multicoloured chaos of the carnival but a clear, white light, glowing steadily.

The caravan. Without thinking, she follows the stars to the caravan's door. The metal is dented and sun-bleached. She goes to knock, and the door opens.

'Martin,' she blurts out, then adds: 'Mark? Michael.' She might not be sure of his name but she's sure it's Albie's missing boy, bulky and broad, with his rectangular rimless glasses and salt-white goatee.

He moves into the light and he's not any more, he's a slight teenage girl, smooth-faced and blue-eyed, draped in a dress like a length of starlight which flutters in a wind that isn't there. Molly blinks in confusion – are they both in there? Is that where he's been, shacked up with some poor teenager in this freezing tin box? She should call the police, she should call his wife.

The girl moves to make space for Molly to come in and she's not any more, she's a man in his thirties, handsome but not intimidatingly so, dark-eyed and dark-haired, looking half like Molly wished she looked and half like her favourite ex-boyfriend.

'Who are you?' she asks, which is the only thing she can think to say.

'Who are you looking for?' The man's voice is soft, with an accent she can't place. He reaches for her hand and she lets him take it. She thought his skin would be cold and clatter like the starfish, but it's warm. He doesn't pull her into the caravan. He doesn't push her away either. He just stands, her hand in his.

'I want –' starts Molly, but she doesn't know how to continue.

'I know you do,' the man says, and his words come out cold, the steam from his breath coiling and distorting like the smoke in the greenhouse, and he blinks and his eyes are white, frozen through.

Molly slides her hand out of his and backs away. He doesn't stop her. Frozen starfish clatter under her heels and she loses her balance, stumbling, twisting, and she turns her face to the funfair lights and she runs without looking back.

The council take away the starfish, though not before they thaw and the seagulls spread many of the half-eaten bodies across the town. The carnival adds a new ride: a small one for children, where you ride on a big plastic caterpillar and it rolls up and down, up and down, and through the hole in a big plastic rotten apple. Dorota's, Cathryn's and Heather's husbands run away; the rumour is they got tangled in a bad investment scheme and emigrated to South America. Winter shifts to spring, to summer.

Pink blossom flutters down as Molly sits in the greenhouse with Liz and Mia. The air is full of the smell of tomato plants, which line the inner walls of the greenhouse along with lettuce, cucumber and sweet peas. Molly doesn't know if all these things should be planted together, or if she'll actually get vegetables from them, but at least the tomatoes smell good and the sweet peas are a dozen shades of pink and purple. She refills Liz's glass.

'There's a questionnaire in here,' says Mia, folding back the covers of her book. 'What's your sex personality? Are you a sexual daredevil or a little more subdued? Do you let yourself go or hold back? What are your notions of sexual normalcy and eccentricity? Are you sexually creative?'

'Are we supposed to be answering these?' Liz sips her drink and pulls a deadhead off a sweet pea, dropping it to the soil.

'I used to be sexually creative,' says Molly. She pokes her foot out of the greenhouse door to catch a falling blossom. 'I met Albie when I worked in a strip club, did I ever tell you that?'

Mia looks up from the book. '*No*. Seriously?'

Molly knows the place in her mind: the blare of 'Pour Some Sugar on Me', the watered-down drinks, the row of lockers containing body glitter and tampons and deodorant. She can feel the ache in her feet from the platform heels, can smell the baby powder she pats on her inner thighs. She's seen it in a dozen films. She knows it's a risk, telling a story to more than one person. The trick is to only ever tell one person at a time, and make sure they won't confer with someone who might have heard a different version. But she couldn't resist; she thought Liz and Mia would like it. And she's right. They're gazing at her, half doubt, half wide-eyed interest.

'Albie saved me,' says Molly.

Liz snorts and rolls her eyes just as Mia says, 'That is so romantic!'

'I had to work there to escape my parents,' says Molly. 'They were rich but negligent and I grew up at an international school in Brussels. And I also grew up in a cult because my parents were religious, but the bad kind. I had a baby and they made me give it up.'

'What the fuck, Molly.' Liz puts down her glass.

'Is that true?' asks Mia.

The breeze shifts, and Molly catches the smell of frying doughnuts. Another pink blossom falls.

'Kidding,' she says, with a smile. 'Or, actually, no, it's that game. Where you say one thing that really happened, and two that you only wish.'

'Who the fuck would wish for any of that?'

Molly doesn't know what she wants to wish for. She could go back to the caravan and knock on the door and see what the shapeshifter has become. Would she prefer to see her child, or her lover?

She thinks the caravan would be colder inside than out. She thinks it would be completely empty, the inner walls smooth and pale, nacreous like the inside of a shell. The tiny windows would be steamed opaque on the outside and everything would gleam pearlescent and Molly would think – if I broke apart one of the frozen starfish, is this what they'd look like inside?

She wants to serve meatballs and tell outrageous lies, and the next night lie in the empty bed and wonder aloud where Albie could possibly be, whether he could have fallen asleep in his car or run off with her from the takeaway. She wants to want something – or the absence of something, of someone – as intensely as the other wives in the town.

'I guess when you don't know what ...' Molly trails off. 'When you don't know what you want, exactly, or you make a wish and it's not really clear, or if you ...' She fiddles with a tomato plant, tugging at an unripe tomato the size of her thumb-tip. 'If you don't know what you want, then the tides change, or the wind, and you get pulled along and you end up ...'

The tomato comes off in her hand and she pops it in her mouth. It's hard and tart and she swallows it without chewing it properly. It hurts going down.

Molly gets out of bed after Albie is asleep, which is a thing she does semi-regularly now, the secret like a bonbon she keeps tucked in her cheek. She goes to the pale shell of the caravan, and knocks, and sees who emerges. They're different every time, but every time she recognises them. Sometimes they shift even as she watches.

She follows them down to the end of the beach, the frothy flotsam part where no one goes because the rock pools are full of what the seagulls won't eat.

Together they wade into the water and swim around the bay, out to a deep cave in the rocks. They dive deep, down, down almost to where the light stops. There's no colour here, no smell, no sound. The water weeds are dark, anchored to the seabed, their fronds thick as forearms and restless in the slow waves.

Tangled up in the weeds are the husbands. They sleep, calm and still, desireless. Molly strokes each of their faces in turn. Not for them the smoky, poky greenhouse and the palm-size slap of cards. Not for them the line of house-street-carnival-sand. Their world here is vast and boundless, unknowable.

The next time Molly sees Dorota and Cathryn and Heather and Mia she could reassure them that their husbands are doing just fine here. But Dorota and Cathryn and Heather and Mia have never asked.

Molly watches the husbands, sleeping still with smiles on their faces, wrapped in the umbilical water weeds, and she thinks: I could ask for this. I could want this. I could wish for it, and I could get it.

Then she thinks: no. This is what I will do. I will go home to Albie, and I will take his hand and lead him to the carnival by the sea.

Together, in the pale light of the morning, she thinks, they will board the Ferris wheel. They will circle and circle until the wheel stops with them at the very height of it. The highest place in the town; the furthest point from the dark water weeds, from the thing that gleams colourless in the deepest part of the sea. He will take her hand and kiss the back of it, absent-minded and gallant, tender and unthinking.

'Want to go round again?' Molly will say, and Albie will nod. They will sit together as the lights flash on their skin. They will wait for the garish flamingo sunrise, the bright yolky day.

Nightfall

The first time she came to me, I woke in blood. My bed was crimson velvet – at least I called it velvet, though of course it was velour, scratchily artificial and bought from some high street discount place in the post-Halloween sale. The man-made whatever-it-was soaked up the blood beautifully so I didn't notice at first that I'd got my period: gushingly so, bright red, flooding out like the elevator in *The Shining*. What I did notice was the suck on my cunt. More specifically, the tongue slipping between my inner labia, the languid drag on my clit. I thought it was a dream – wanted it to be a dream – was afraid it was a dream. I kept my eyes closed. The room was too hot and smelled like rotting flowers. I felt teeth. A blissful, burning pull. The jab of a forked tongue. I came, hard, in a hot gush of blood, and I felt my whole body convulse and pulse and pulse and she climbed on top of me and lay her body on mine, the sweet weight of her, her cool clean skin on every part of my skin, and by the time I could open my eyes it was all gone: the blood, the throb, the night, the oxytocin, her.

The morning sun felt sour. I could smell my mother burning the toast.

The menagerie of crystal animals by my bed had all fallen over. The lilac crystal deer, the size of my clit, had fallen and lay nestled in a light fuzz of dust on the plush carpet. I picked it up and swallowed it.

In the library, I doodled cobwebs on the corner of my notebook. Clouds and a crescent moon. A heart pierced with an arrow. I glanced over at Thessaly's homework and it was just Keir Keir Keir, Thessaly Byrne-Burke, Mrs Byrne-Burke, T+K. Milagro's homework I couldn't see because she'd fallen asleep leaning over it with her head on her arms.

Boys think they know what girls want: an inverse of their own needs. Where they desire, girls want to be desired. Where they want to penetrate something, girls want to be penetrated. Where they hunger, girls want to provide for them. You have to laugh. Poor things. They have no idea of the ferocity in a girl, the ravening wolves pulling in opposite directions.

No idea that a girl can want to be the passive fuck-toy, hypnotised and hogtied, body pulsing as she's penetrated. And at the same time want to be the one penetrating, the one powerful, the rock star, the fuckboy, a lanky seven-foot devil up on a stage humping a mic stand while girls scream until their throats bleed. And at the same time want to be soft, pulpy, clothed in pale velvets, adorned with flowers and worshipped with a dozen gently lapping tongues. And that she can feel all those experiences at the same time during one ordinary morning wank. The thought that one man with one penis could possibly provide that. What a joke.

That was the inside of my mind, the hidden part of me; when on the surface I was pure and clean and doing my Advanced Higher Physics homework. Rotational motion. A little bit of electromagnetism.

It was late closing on a winter evening and the library was saving on lights. The darkness at the end of the corridor said no one else had been here in a while, or if they had then they weren't moving. Sitting in the dark, holding their breath and their tongue. Waiting.

'What's the best thing a guy ever did to you?' said Milagro from the nest of her arms, her voice muffled from her school jumper.

'Left me alone,' I muttered, and I didn't think Milagro had heard but she snorted a laugh.

'With me? Or for me?' said Thessaly. Her jaw worked rhythmically, a fast heartbeat, and she blew a big red bubble and let it pop against her glossed lips.

Milagro's head jerked up. She looked confused. 'No, *to* you. You know.'

'Keir always says he'll kill me if I leave him.'

'Oh my God,' Milagro breathed, eyes wide. 'You're so lucky.'

I think all girls want to be a little bit killed. But only a little.

Milagro was still staring enviously at Thessaly, and Thessaly was toying with this tiny gold pendant she wears – we all have them, it's a theme, she has a guillotine, Milagro has the thumbscrews, and I have the pear of anguish. We'd started with the standard instrument-of-torture accessory, the crucifix, but we liked to branch out, because we were not like other girls, just like all girls say.

I went to say something, I don't know what now, maybe that thing about being killed but only a little, and something caught in my throat and I sneezed and a fine red mist of blood landed like dandelion fluff on the desk between us.

Thessaly shrieked and yanked her books off the desk. The movement triggered the lights and they all flickered on.

'Not again,' I said, tipping my head back. I felt the blood drip metallic down the back of my throat.

It happened fairly regularly - still happens, sometimes. Thin skin somewhere inside me, not enough to keep my insides inside.

'Did I get blood on you?' I sounded like I was speaking through a gag.

'No, it's just...' Thessaly sounded awkward. 'It was just a surprise. It's not like I think you're gross or anything. It's not that. It's just, the blood and stuff, that's how you get diseases.'

Milagro gasped. I still had my head tipped back, so I could feel rather than see that she was glaring at Thessaly.

'Faith, oh my God, oh my God,' said Thessaly, awkwardly patting my shoulder. 'So stupid, I'm sooooo sorry. I didn't even think about your brother. Did I make you sad? Do you think you'll cry?'

Christian is five years older than me and I haven't seen him in almost that same amount of time. My mother was too angry at him leaving to ask herself why he did.

When the blood seemed to have slowed, I did a big sniff. A gelatinous clot of blood hit my throat and I swallowed it silently, not even gagging.

'I don't think he caught it from a sneeze,' I said. Probably a cock, possibly a needle.

At a sleepover once I woke to a sex-like stickiness on my lip and cheeks, and found blood gushing from my nose. I don't know why my first thought was to turn to Kerensa Byrne-Burke - whose house we were staying at, and who had heard me shifting in my sleeping bag and had also sat up - and grin, knowing that my teeth would be bloodied. I liked the thought that I was a still from a horror movie poster. I don't know if I thought Kerensa was going to kiss me, or laugh, or run away screaming, and I don't know which I wanted. In any case, she just stared at me, and I went wordlessly to the bathroom and spat a gloppy red clot into the toilet bowl, right on the shit smears her older brother had left. Unless it wasn't him, and it was Kerensa; everyone shits, after all, even posh girls. Maybe especially posh girls.

After I woke up bleeding a few times, my mother decided it was time I stopped, and she took me to the hospital, to a strange below-ground department with extremely bright lights and fake birdsong piped in and a smell of bleach and pollen. There a nurse put hot needles up my nose to cauterise... something, I don't know exactly what. It didn't hurt. I still taste blood some mornings, but now it only goes back into me, and never out, like the nurse put up a little construction barrier. The building of my body is still crumbling, but I can't see it, so I guess who cares.

She's like that, my mother. Always a barrier. I know it sounds dramatic to say but I don't think she's touched me since I was a baby. Even then, she told me that when she fed me and Christian, she had to use these plastic nipple shields, because we wouldn't latch on properly. But I think it's so that no part of her had to touch us. It's safer that way, I know. A placenta so our bloods didn't have to touch. Rubber gloves. Hair nets. Face masks. Condoms.

'Wash your pad,' my mother said when she found the packet in the bathroom cabinet. I hadn't even told her I'd got my period; I just went to the pharmacy. 'Wash it off in the sink and then wash the sink.'

'And then what do I do with it?'

My mother wrinkled her nose like I had just thrust my bloody pad under it.

'Then throw it away.'

'Then why wash it, if I'm going to throw it away?'

She took a deep breath and exhaled slowly, like I was getting on her last nerve, and breathing techniques were all that was standing between her and murder. The brand of pad I bought had the tagline '... Because.' Because what? Because I'm shedding womb lining? Because blood is gushing from my vagina? Even the period pad people couldn't bring themselves to say 'period'.

That's all my mother ever told me about periods: wash it away, throw it away. She didn't tell me that at first it would look like I had shat myself. She didn't tell me it could be ropey or mucousy or come out of me in clots. She didn't tell me that my cramps would feel like there was an enormous pepper grinder, slow with rust, twisting inside me. She didn't tell me it would smell like raw steak or like old pennies or like rotten eggs. Just: get rid of it, and don't let anyone know.

She didn't need to tell me why, because I already knew. I knew who - what - wanted young girls' blood. I'd read plenty of books where the girls wanted to give it to them, too. And there's only one way to give someone a lot of your blood without hurting yourself. The books didn't say the vampires liked periods in particular, because no one ever says that word. But I knew. '... Because.'

I didn't have a tissue to wipe my blood off the desk, and I didn't want to get it on the library books or my school uniform. I thought about licking it up, or using my hair, but Thessaly and Milagro were watching me. I remembered the morning and wondered if I'd shit out that little crystal deer whole, or if it would shatter inside me, or my body would absorb it entirely.

'Come on,' I said, and picked up my books without touching the blood. 'We'll miss the bus.'

That night my period was in full flow and she sucked the blood from me over and over and over and over and over and over. She whispered things to me, about how I was her slut, her toy, her doll, how she owned me, how I was just a thing to her, how I made her want to hurt me; she whispered it all in my ear, voice thick as cream and dense with love. Afterwards she crawled up my body and held me until I stopped shaking.

In English we were reading *Dracula*, because of course we were. Girl gangs dress to theme, so Thessaly was in a red veil stitched with tiny black seed pearls, Milagro had walked down the corridor holding a lit candle so the wax spilled and hardened on her hand, and under my uniform I was wearing a belt of rose thorns (plastic, sadly, but it still pricked). Obviously Miss St Cyr made them put the veil and candle in their bags, and also Milagro had to go and run her hands under the cold tap and take a detention for having an open flame in school, and that's why I'm smarter than Thessaly and Milagro, because no one knew I had my thorns on.

Keir Byrne-Burke, with the same pale eyes and underbite as his twin Kerensa, was reading. His seat was beside mine and I could smell him: feet, washing powder, cum. It was the bit with the vampire brides and he'd already read 'wicked burning desire that they would kiss me with those red lips' and he'd even managed 'deliberate voluptuousness', but 'languorous ecstasy' was obviously too much for him, and he stumbled over the words, and I didn't notice because I'd read on ahead and was thinking about my own languorous ecstasy, tilting my hips so my labia pressed my clit against the hard plastic chair, and I brought my thumb to my mouth and pressed my teeth down on it, ripping off a loose edge of skin, and the tiniest salt of blood burst on my tongue and I must have made a sound then because Keir Byrne-Burke was on his feet, his back to the rest of the class so only I could see the hard-on carbuncle in his trousers.

'Fuck you laughing at, fucking cunt,' he said, big man, big tough man, leaning over my desk and getting his spit on my book.

'Keir,' said Miss St Cyr, and I wish I could say it was in a warning tone, but she mostly just sounded tired. 'Sit back down. The word is pronounced *languorous*.'

'Your brother,' said Keir, bringing his face close to mine, his voice low, almost a growl, like a motor trying to start, 'your fucking brother fucked filth and now he's fucking dead. That's what you get. Because –'

And he didn't get any further, because I girlishly tilted my head up towards him, or I suppose not so much a tilt as a very hard nod, a head-butt, some might say, and his nose burst into blood and so did mine, and the surprise of it made me laugh and the blood on my lips sprayed right into Keir's face.

'Fuck!' he was shouting, backing away from me, bumping into desks, frantically swiping my blood off his face. 'Fuck! Help! Fuck!'

I turned to Milagro, who had been toying with her gold thumb-screws necklace, and I expected her to laugh too but she scraped back her desk and moved away from me, still holding the tiny thumbscrews like she was warding back a demon.

In the toilets I ran my hands under the cold tap. There wasn't actually that much blood. It had dried in a row of drips from my nose, round the curve of my mouth and down my throat. A row of rubies. What a waste that we only put jewels on our ears and throat; the colour looked so pretty there.

I heard the door open and Milagro came in. I didn't turn to look at her; just at her reflection in the spit-smeared mirror. She looked ugly, reflected. Her hands were scalded red from the candle wax.

'Keir is such a dick,' she said. 'He deserved that. I wasn't on his side or anything, I just got a shock. You'd think I'd be used to the sight of blood by now, you'd think all girls would be, isn't it weird that we're meant to be like these delicate –'

'I don't have anything,' I said to her reflection. 'In my blood.'

'I know, God, I know, it's just, the other day, what Thessaly said. About that's how you get diseases. It was on my mind, and I – Faith, I'm trying to apologise, are you even listening?'

I handed her the wet paper towel, blood still smeared down my throat. She stood there, mouth open, until it dawned on her. For a second I thought she was going to clean me up, but she mumbled something about being late for French, and dropped the paper towel in the bin on her way out.

She came to me again that night and she said to me: 'Shall I tell you that I love you?' She leaned in and pressed her nose to my throat, a slow inhale, and I felt a part of me go inside her. 'No. That's not it. You want me to say: I hate you.' She pulled the blood from me then, a little from my nose and a little from my thumb and then it was my cunt, my cunt, my cunt, and though her mouth was full I still heard her words in my head, her voice deep inside me, I hate you, I hate you, I hate you, and I came so hard I scraped my throat raw. That morning I had put my tiny crystal rabbit in my mouth and rolled it around. It fit perfectly between my upper teeth. I had a deer, a rabbit, a turtle, a mouse, a sparrow. I had only just noticed that all my crystal animals were prey.

I lay there under her and I wondered what would happen if you could gather all your dark things. If you could bring all the shadows in you together, crush them all in your hands. What would you get? A blank space, a compressed nothingness? Or would it be better and

71

richer, the best and most delicious parts of you, the boiled-down essence?

A few days later my period finished. I told myself I could wait. My period would come again – that's what they did, they were known for it. Every single month, the pepper-grinder wretchedness, the judder of the dry tampon, watching the blood pool and pink around your feet in the shower. Worrying that you smell like past-its-sell-by mince. Worrying that you actually quite like that smell.

In the library with all the lights gone to dark except mine, I read about night terrors. I read about a man who tried to be rid of his night terrors by bleeding himself regularly. It didn't say what he did with the blood, whether he ate it or threw it away or what. It did say that the bleeding had the opposite effect, the incubus being 'aggravated rather than abated', so he doubled the amount of the blood-draw. I wondered if two incubi came to him then, and if he was tempted to triple it to call three, or if he was scared of losing too much blood, and dying.

I lingered on the description of being ridden by the night hag, the sinister figure made of shadows, the sensation of being suffocated, the feeling of being pinned down, the impossibility of escape, and I felt my stomach twist like a period cramp and my clit throbbed and I pressed against the seam of my jeans and with tiny movements I made myself come in silence at my desk.

The next morning I got up and rinsed the crusts from my eyes with icy water. Pulled my hair into a ponytail. Clenched my teeth until I felt a back one squeal and almost crack. Applied my SPF and my acne gel. Punched myself in the mouth. Tasted blood.

I never asked her to come to me. I never consented. Boys make you say yes but you don't know what you're saying yes to, and once you've said it then it's too late. You consent to their grubby hands on you, their hangnails scratching your vaginal walls. You consent to a cheesy pissy cock in your mouth. You consent to it going inside you, squishy and solid at the same time, like a hard-boiled egg. You say you want to because that's what they want to hear. You don't get to actually want things, you only get to say the word.

With her, I agreed to nothing, and got exactly what I wanted.

My period came back early, two weeks later, as if it couldn't wait. The soft clock of my body, losing time. It happened suddenly, in a way it didn't usually, like a plug had been yanked out. I was in the shower and a clot plopped out of me and nuzzled into the arch of my foot. Usually I'd rinse it away without looking, but this time I squatted down and poked at it. It was viscous, substantial, somewhere between jam and egg yolk. I squatted there in the shower, the steam rising up around me, and I felt my body open and release, and I felt alive, like the animal I was.

In bed I rolled out the red carpet for her. I thought about making a joke about that but that would involve speaking and I don't think she wants me to speak. I made a noise once, a feral grunt that could have been *more* or *no* or *why*, I don't even know, I wasn't thinking in words at that point, and she slipped her cold dry fingers into my mouth to silence me.

'When you die,' she said to me that night, 'I will fuck you one more time then feed you to wolves,' and I think where the hell is she going to find wolves, and then I think about how I heard about rewilding, about wolves being reintroduced in the north of Scotland, and I think about a wolf snout parting my labia, fur against my fur, a wolf tooth sliding against my clit, the smell of blood and meat, the death of something weaker than me, and I came again.

I thought about how when I die, she will take her sharp pinkie nail and slice me open from my throat to my cunt and spread me wide. She will take out all my glistening purple innards and put them in their own individual dishes. Perhaps the dishes will be crystal. I think they will gleam.

My period came and went and came and went and it wasn't enough, it was never enough.

I peeled off scabs and she came to me.

I ripped off hangnails and she came to me.

I violently waxed my pubic hair and she came to me.

I cut lines into my thighs with a razor and she came to me.

I jabbed a compass into the soft flesh behind my ear and she came to me.

I called her, and she came, and so did I, over and over and over, and she kissed me with her tongue hot and bloody and I tasted myself, and I was held and I was cleansed and I was still.

One day after school I went to Mädchen's house, because I love Mädchen's house. She's Milagro's mum and so Milagro is there too and that's fine, even though things are weird between us kind of, she never said anything about that day in the school toilets and neither did I, but we can still sprawl on the mauve inflatable chairs in her room and tip sugar into our mouths and use her magenta lips phone to call boys, because what else is there to do?

Mädchen's kitchen is like a witch's kitchen, steaming warm, herbs and copper pots everywhere. I was very pale by then, and I felt hungry and sick all the time, and the heat in the kitchen made my head spin. Black curtains seemed to swoop in at the edge of my vision like I was on a theatre stage and the show was over, it was time to go, but then the blackness receded like they had changed their mind and I had to do an encore.

In the kitchen Mädchen was stirring batter in a bowl with a wooden spoon, with all these ornate glasses set out, full of something dark. Milagro dumped her bag and coat on the floor, then picked up a glass and sniffed it.

'I wouldn't drink that,' said Mädchen lightly. 'It's blood.'

'Gross, Mum, ugh! Why?'

'For the brownies.'

'Blood brownies? Grossness. Where did you even get it?'

'You've eaten these many times, my pet, and have never complained. The blood gives it the perfect texture. Crumbly and fudgy.'

'I wish I didn't know what was in them. I can't eat them now.'

'Can I?' I asked. The glasses were so beautiful, tiny and all different colours, etched with stars. They were probably vintage. They were probably from some really cool shop that only Mädchen knew about.

She smiled. 'Of course you can. The iron will be good for you. Are you menstruating? Milagro just finished.'

'Mum, God, can you not?'

'You girls need to pay attention to your iron. I know all about it. Oh, how I bled!'

Milagro flounced out of the room, her steps thud-thud-thudding up the stairs, and with a grin Mädchen offered me the spoon to lick. She was right; the blood really did make it syrupy. I pressed the batter to the roof of my mouth with my tongue, feeling the crystals of sugar dissolve.

'I had fibroids and I bled through everything! Pads as thick as steaks - two of them - and still I bled through,' said Mädchen. She winked at me and then licked the spoon herself. If she'd taken care not to lick the same part I had, she didn't make it obvious. But I noticed she put it in the sink after, and took a fresh spoon to her batter. 'Need something bigger,' she said, and I don't know if she meant the spoon or her pads. 'I left trails of blood on the floor, on the furniture. I felt, all the time, as if I'd just stood up from a very hot bath. Everything had a sort of light mist through it, the edges fuzzy. Like being in a dream all the time.'

'Do you miss it?' My voice was quiet, muffled by the gooey batter.

'Oh, it's not over for me! Not, at least –' and here she came close to me and whispered theatrically in my ear, even though no one except the cat and the blood could hear us, '– at least as far as my husband is concerned. I put a tiny bit of raw liver in my panties every month. Can't have him thinking I'm old!'

'I thought men didn't like periods. The boys at school say it's disgusting. They say they can smell our pads.'

'That is just boys. A real man appreciates that a woman is most sacred when she is bleeding.'

Mädchen is a midwife. She spends every day literally looking at vaginas and the things that come out of them. She told me once that when pregnant women call to say stuff has come out of them, she gets them to bring the stuff in, even if it's messy or it smells. The midwives put on white gloves and examine the stuff with their fingers, discussing the colour and texture, the give and collapse of it. They stretch it out and rub it between finger and thumb. She said they smell it. I wanted to ask if they ever taste it, but I thought even for Mädchen that was too far. That was before I saw her little glasses of blood. I don't think they're from her work, though I didn't ask, and she didn't tell.

Mädchen stopped and looked at me. She tucked my hair behind my ear and gently, so gently, stroked the scabbed-over cuts. She cupped my face in her hands, her wrist bones on my collarbones, her fingertips over my ears, and she kissed me on the forehead.

'Faith,' she said, 'you shouldn't let anyone hurt you.'

'You don't understand,' I said.

'I know,' said Mädchen. 'I know.'

I helped her bake the brownies and, later, despite what she'd said, Milagro did eat them. They were delicious.

In the library all the lights were off except the one on me. I was wearing my pear of anguish and my belt of rose thorns and reading about the signs someone has been visited by a vampire: fatigue, lethargy, loss of appetite or extreme hunger, insomnia or hypersomnia, excessive passion or listlessness, unexpected bloodstains. Common symptoms of menstruation: fatigue, lethargy, loss of appetite or extreme hunger...

We used to play a game, Thessaly and Milagro and me. One girl would put her hands around another girl's throat and find the biggest vein, then press on it. The blood would start to pound, you could hear it throb in your ears, like being underwater in a storm, and you'd have to look her in the eye until you passed out. We thought some kind of truth would be caught there in our eyes, like crystal balls. I can't remember when we stopped playing that game.

I feel bad about this story. About all of it. Shouldn't it be a girl-power narrative? Isn't it all about girl power now? Shouldn't I be empowered and strong and good and sort of relatable too, with a minor adorable flaw like a bad singing voice or always being late?

But it's my choice. It's my power. If it's my choice, then how can it be damage? If it gets me what I want, then isn't that power?

Mädchen was only trying to be kind. But she should have known that a bit of liver in her knickers could solve her problems, but it wouldn't do shit for mine.

I spread myself on my crimson velvet bed and I opened my best vein as wide as I could. I knew she would come to me, lie on me and take from me – but it wasn't like before.

She was inside me. All the way.

Wrapping around my bones, ribboning through my muscles and sinew. It was agony.

I gasped out and came harder than I ever had – than I ever have, to this day, despite the attempts of many lovers and professionals – and I felt her come with me.

And I think I died. I really think I died.

That was the last time.

I woke to a paramedic's mouth pressed to mine. The lights were very bright. I was freezing cold and very white, and there was no blood anywhere. The cut on my wrist looked puffy and puckered, like I'd been underwater for a long time.

My mother held my hand tight. When I opened my eyes and looked at her, she raised my hand and kissed it so hard I felt her teeth through her lips.

'Faith,' she said, and pulled me close to her. 'Oh, Faith.'

She held me like that for maybe thirty seconds, her heart beating against mine, her nose pressed to my hair, and then the paramedic had me sit up so she could check my blood pressure and my mother never touched me again.

I turned eighteen and I wasn't dead, and neither was Christian, so I went to live with him. Plenty of people hurt me, including me, but no one ever did it as carefully as she did.

It's been many years since she came to me. I'm not a girl now and I have made another body inside mine and birthed it in a wave of agony and blood and then a few years later I did it all again and I pushed so hard that it felt like all my glistening innards fell right out and every drop of blood in me was gone and even then, even then, she never came back. She never came back to me.

I still have the scars, soft and silver, touchable and tender, the most beautiful part of me; a reminder that once, once, I was loved.

Privilege

ietra got ready in the bathroom because it was the room she hated the most. Or would that be the master bedroom? The orangery, maybe? The second study? She had such a wealth of choice.

The bath and sink were marble, a style called Rosso Laguna, deep red with grey veins, which looked to her like huge slabs of steak. There were mirrors on all the walls. An endless meat room.

She waxed her bikini line. She always put it on a little too hot. Counted to three, then ripped. She liked the feeling after, those breathless seconds before it started to throb. As she watched, the bare chickenish skin beaded with blood. She didn't know if it was meant to do that but didn't know how to stop it happening. Perhaps it was that she struggled to get a decent grip on the wax sheet. No one's fault but her own.

From a distant room, a thud. Something falling; she didn't go to investigate. There was always something that needed to be propped up, repainted, trimmed back. She pressed a damp cloth to her labia and waited for the bleeding to slow. Her husband had bought the house. With her family's money, mostly, but he chose it. A project for her. A treat. Something to keep her occupied. Busywork for her mild and meaningless life.

At first she'd agreed. It was an important house. *Historically* important. She was part of something that mattered. Every change to the house required masses of paperwork and permissions, and she'd liked that too; liked signing her name over and over, an autograph.

She removed the cloth, the blood smearing. It was fine. She'd put some nappy rash cream on and hope for the best.

She'd joked with her husband that the Rosso Laguna was a good investment. Marble lasts for centuries. When she was dead, they could hack the bathroom counters out to make her headstone. He hadn't laughed, but she suspected that if she died before him, he'd remember and seriously consider it.

The bedroom walls were marble too. Not real marble; there was some reason, some bit of paperwork that meant they couldn't be, the centuries-old walls or the floor wouldn't support the weight in that part of the house. Instead she'd been instructed to make it look like marble by drawing lines with a soft pencil and slightly smudging them with a velvet cloth. The lines shouldn't be too straight or too curved but should look, said a needlessly precious website, like the gently meandering tracks of rain down a windowpane.

Her hands already ached, and she hadn't even done her mascara or blow-dried her hair yet. She ran her hands under the hot tap to loosen the crooked knuckles, but the water came in cold. It only took a minute to numb her fingers completely.

'It must be a real privilege,' the man said, his jaw chiselled, his aftershave cloying, his latte, horribly, barely even begun.

Pietra tried again. She regretted starting. Not just this story, not just this Tinder date, not just her failed marriage, not just the house, not just her adult life, but everything, all of it.

'The thing is,' she said, 'even the stream at the bottom of the garden is protected. They sent me a leaflet telling me what I can and can't let grow around it. I have to buy certain plants, and pay for them myself. I can't feed the voles, but I can't let them die either. They asked me to count the ladybirds.'

He'd put his hand on the table between them, at the midpoint. She read in *Grazia* that's an invitation, a respectful courtship: not invading her half of the table, but not keeping only to his half either. She knew she could reach out and take his hand, but instead she held on to her espresso cup, already empty. If she kept her fingers pressed together, they didn't look crooked. She didn't know if she was playing hard to get, an expert in the dating game; or she just couldn't bear to even acknowledge this game, never mind play it.

'Incredible,' he said, and finally, mercifully, sipped some of his latte. She looked at the line it made on the glass, willing it to go down, like when she'd lived in a flat share and felt penned lines on her milk, wanting to catch her flatmate stealing it so she had a reason to yell. 'What a privilege,' he said. 'A real privilege. I can't imagine.'

He sipped again and grimaced; the coffee was bad, or that's just what his face looked like. The cafe was playing the *Ally McBeal* theme tune; if she'd been asked ten minutes ago what the *Ally McBeal* theme tune is, she wouldn't have had a clue, but there it was, and she instantly knew it. She wanted to say to him: well, could you *try* to imagine? Could you just fucking try?

'It took me two weeks to draw those fake marble lines on the walls in pencil. Two full weeks, and that's working weekends too, and evenings if it wasn't too dark. And when he got home from his work trip, he didn't even notice.' She might as well have shat in her hand and smeared it on the walls, for all the difference it made, she thought but didn't say.

Pietra's mother did that once. Not on purpose. In the big supermarket. She felt it coming and slipped her hand down the back of her Chanel skirt suit and caught it. It was small and hard and didn't smell much; this was because she was always dehydrated and ate mostly persimmons, both in a bid to remain thin. She'd been retired from dancing for over two decades by then, but still retained a prima ballerina's figure, despite her three children. She used that word a lot when talking about her children: *despite*. She straightened her skirt and held her full hand casually by her side. She'd never taken her other hand off the trolley.

The toilet was in the far corner, near the exit. She was in the opposite corner, in the bakery. Perhaps the smell of the bread was what had brought it on. Apparently the smell of books can do that; she'd read about it recently in a magazine article, libraries and bookshops could both bring it on, the uncontrollable urge. Some kind of chemical in the ink, or the tendency to squat to look at books on the lower shelves, perhaps. She hadn't squatted. And she didn't even eat bread. It was for the children's lunches. She made her way to the far corner.

But the problem was Sophie from the next village. And then Rachelle from the club. And then Imogen whose son, David or Daniel – perhaps she had two, David *and* Daniel – had been round for dinner with her own son a few times. 'I must tell you about the church fete,' they said, 'it's a scandal, it really is, and nothing will be done about it,' and she didn't want to admit she didn't give a stuff about the church fete, that she didn't even go to church, she hadn't even had the children christened. 'Do say hello to your husband,' they said, and she wondered if they'd forgotten his name, which was understandable. 'And how *are* the children?' they said, and usually she'd rankle at the odd emphasis, as if the children would be anything other than small gods walking the earth, miniature miracles she'd produced with her own body.

But she was distracted. The thing in her hand had grown cold. She tried to hold her fingers loosely so it wouldn't squish through, but not so loosely it could fall out. Though perhaps if it did she could kick it quickly under the refrigerated units without anyone noticing. She shuffled closer to the cheese section, ready to relax her hand, ready to casually kick out her foot.

That was always the end of the story. Pietra's mother had told it several times, but always broke off there, laughing at the thought of herself kicking a little nugget of shit under the cottage cheese. Probably she made it to the toilet and flushed and washed without anyone knowing. Possibly the whole thing had never happened at all. Or possibly her small shit was still there, lost under the refrigerated units, deep inside the supermarket, fossilised, a coprolite.

There were other people in the cafe where Pietra agreed to meet the man. People on laptops, people artfully photographing their muffins, people coaxing scraps of toast into their offspring.

'There's a statue in the centre of the hedge maze,' she said. 'A sphinx. Do you know what a sphinx is?' The man smiled and sipped his latte, then grimaced again. 'It was very damaged by the weather,' she said. 'Almost entirely eroded; you could barely tell what it was. I worked so hard to restore it, and it looked great, and it was a privilege to do that work, it really was.' She went to sip her own coffee before remembering it was finished. She forced her face into a smile. She could taste his aftershave. 'I took it out of the maze and put it in prime place in the garden, so you could see it from the French doors. It looked great. The haunches lion-like, the wings bird-like, the head and the breasts...'

The head, actually, was very like hers, and the breasts too, she'd thought. And she hadn't made it like that. It was already like that, underneath all the moss and bird shit. Her face, but smoother. Expressionless. Ready to present a riddle and then tear a man to pieces with her claws, or cast herself off a mountainside in despair, depending. She was familiar with sphinxes from her Classics degree, but she'd looked them up on Wikipedia anyway. She waited for him to say that it was a real privilege, but he just held his latte glass and smiled benignly at her. He was probably thinking about breasts. Men liked breasts, she knew that much, even if they were on eroded statues of sphinxes.

'The thing is,' she went on. 'The thing is that everyone thought it was a hare. A hare! Everyone who came round for dinner, work friends, neighbours, everyone, said: *what a beautiful hare.* Not the sphinx with its questions and its danger, but prey. A pretty little prey. Isn't that funny?'

He laughed obediently and mumbled something, again, about privilege. She wanted to say to him, to scream at him: can't you see? Can't you see the incredible burden of all this? Can't you see that all these business trips and Fallow & Bore sample pots and casual dinners for fifteen of your work colleagues are like sacks of rubble on my back? Can't you see that it's all so heavy, just so fucking heavy, and I don't know how to get out from under it all?

*

Her parents wanted her to be a pianist. It fit in nicely with their careers: the retired ballerina and her much younger actor husband. She taught at a dance school, mostly children. He'd done small plays, the occasional TV show; though he was always a minor character, never the lead. Often he was the murderer in a crime-of-the-week show. If you watched a lot of these types of shows, which Pietra did, he was immediately identifiable, as he appeared to be just an uncle of the victim, just a neighbour, just a guy from work; but he was on-screen a little too long and spoke lines that were a little too unusual, and also didn't you recognise the actor from something?

Over the years his roles dropped away, and he devoted himself full-time to creating a museum of Kirstie Allsopp memorabilia. This had started with the usual signed photos and annotated scripts, but expanded to include the entire contents of her kitchen - including spatulas and chipped Le Creuset stock pots and an egg slicer - which seemed to Pietra a strange thing to have been put on sale as Kirstie Allsopp wasn't known for cooking especially and also she wasn't even dead. She wondered if Kirstie Allsopp had bought a new egg slicer to replace that one, or if she was glad to be rid of it.

He needed to get just the right kind of display cases and couldn't open the museum until he had them. He put pine cones on the seats of Kirstie Allsopp's dining chairs, so that no one would sit on them. The smaller items were stacked in disintegrating boxes in the stables. He seemed very sure that people would pay to visit the Kirstie Allsopp museum, when it was ready, and the location and disrepair of their remote farmhouse would be no impediment.

Pietra's fingers were long and strong. Her mother loved them. She'd described them as pianist's hands since Pietra was a toddler; she found them Pietra's most beautiful feature, and although she never said it, Pietra knew they were the only valuable or unusual thing about her.

When she was sent away to boarding school at twelve years old, Pietra found herself sitting on her hands. The wooden benches were hard and her hands, squashed between the boards and her thighs, soon went numb. She kept sitting on them, for hours at a time, until the numbness grew to an ache and then into a sharp and pleasant agony and then back to numbness again. When she eventually stood up, her hands were as white as eggs and hung uselessly from her wrists. It took a long time for the feeling to come back into her fingers, but it always did.

She broke a few by slamming them in a door, then another by getting into a fight with another girl, then a few more with a hammer alone behind the greenhouse after lights-out. She once overheard her father on the phone saying that he'd stayed with Pietra's mother for the sake of the children, but they'd all turned out to be disappointments, so it wasn't worth it.

Her fingers healed twisted and weak. Still usable for holding espresso cups or pencilling fake marble lines on walls, but not for playing the piano.

Later, after he had finished his coffee, Pietra fucked the man. It felt strange to fuck sober. Not just sober, but over-caffeinated, hyper-alert. She didn't want to do it in the bedroom because that's where she pencilled the fake marble lines on the walls and either he'd remember that and feel the need to comment on them, to say that they look great or agree that they don't look quite right, not quite convincing, or he wouldn't remember at all and she'd realise that, again, she could have just shat in her hand and smeared it on the wall and it wouldn't have mattered, he'd still have sipped his latte and loomed his aftershave at her and politely, mediocrely fucked her.

She took him instead into the bathroom. She didn't know if she wanted him to comment on the Rosso Laguna or not. He didn't. His inept fingers rubbing two inches above her clitoris, his neatly trimmed chest hair audibly crunching against her breasts, his long narrow penis jabbing her cervix. She closed her eyes so she couldn't see his pale back in the wall-to-wall mirrors, pumping shamefully. She thought of the sphinx. Its spreading wings and strong haunches and bitter expression. It struck her suddenly that she never restored the claws. No claws, but no hands either. The sphinx's arms just ended in weather-worn blobs. She tried to think of some riddles, in case she was ever asked.

The Rosso Laguna was fake. Like the bedroom walls, it looked fine from a distance, but as soon as you touched it, the illusion broke. It was just stick-on sheets, carefully applied with tongs and a spatula to push out air bubbles. At the time she'd seen it as a rebellion. She'd taken the money set aside for the real marble and spent it all on very expensive cocaine from a dealer who dropped unsubtle hints about the names of his celebrity clients. After he left she'd looked at the cocaine in its little bags for a long time before flushing it all down the toilet. A little bit got on her twisted pinkie finger and without thinking she sucked it into her mouth. She waited a while but felt nothing. It looked like icing sugar. Perhaps it was icing sugar. She'd only bought it because it was expensive and easily destroyed.

There was so much she could have done with that money. She could have given it to a homeless person or a food bank. She could have made an anonymous donation to an animal rescue shelter. She could have paid someone to fuck her properly.

Why hadn't she just said no? To the piano, to the house, to the date? But you can't really, can you? You can't just say no.

He still hadn't come and her vagina was dry and raw now so she took him in her hands until he finished. It hurt her knuckles a bit, but no more than anything else. She tried to look aroused but it didn't matter as he had his eyes closed. He came on her belly. It seemed like he was about to apologise, but then he didn't. It had been a daytime date; it wasn't even 3 p.m. It would still be light outside.

She supposed it was a privilege, really. To have a home with a choice of rooms to fuck in, rooms that were all empty since her husband ran off with a woman called Bunny he met on the internet, since he left her alone with her hare and her fake marble and the cooling semen on her belly and the awkward shifting of the stranger beside her. A real privilege.

Wonder

Sarah

The performance was thus, because that is how the men required it: Sarah and Rose were in love. They met on a wrought-iron bench in the park, sitting at opposite ends, every inch of skin covered except their eyes, their skirts so voluminous they couldn't help but touch. They each carried fans, which they used to hide their faces, to coyly glance at one another, and to cool themselves, for it was a hot day.

Or at least, the make-believe was that the day was hot, as later this would give them a reason to remove first one layer of clothing, and then another, and so on; but of course the day outside this room meant nothing, as in here it was perpetually an overheated summer night, the velvets always drawn over the windows, the grandfather clock thudding heavily the seconds, the fires always stoked high, the skin gleaming with sweat, dripping down between their legs so that when the men finally uncovered the hidden petals they could convince themselves that the wetness was their own doing.

Whores in love. A cliché, but what man on heat ever disliked a cliché? The schoolmistress with the whipping cane, the schoolgirl with

91

the pleading eyes, the unfulfilled wife begging to be filled. The menu tended to be somewhat limited, even in this building of surprising bodies and their surprising capabilities.

Sarah adjusted her expression under her veil. The men watching knew that one of the women was one type of wonder, and the other another; but they did not know which was which. Soon enough, they would. Sarah resisted the urge to check she had not let one of the curly golden tendrils escape from her hat or veil or gloves. She wondered what Rose was sitting on, if anything.

Rose had a special skill, which was that she could hold any manner of things inside herself without it showing on the outside. Anything you would like to give to her, she would keep. The only house rules were that it should be nothing sharp or dirty, because they might make Rose unwell or damaged; and that it should be nothing living, because Rose thought it cruel.

Sarah's skill could not rightly be called such. It was not something she had practised or learned; it was something she had been born with.

The first time they were alone together, bathing themselves in rose-water before the men arrived, Sarah had expressed admiration for Rose's vagina and its capacities, but Rose had scoffed. Any woman could do it, she claimed. She merely had to want to. Most women had no idea of what they could hide inside themselves.

'But you,' said Rose wonderingly, 'you are a wonder. A real freak.'

Rose knew that Sarah was not unique; she had seen both of Sarah's sisters. She knew that Sarah was not the most beautiful of the sisters, nor the most thickly pelted. She was merely the middle one, caught between fierceness and loveliness. Yet the way that Rose had called her a wonder made her feel that, perhaps, she might really mean it. Sarah blinked hard, not sure if she was concealing an eye-roll or blinking back tears. How foolish to fall for the trickeries of a whore. As if every man who had ever been alone with Rose did not believe that he was special.

Sarah peeled off her glove, the reveal provoking a series of sounds from the room: a gasp, a chuckle, a groan. She kept her hand in a loose fist to hide the naked pink skin of her palms; it was one of the few truly bare parts of her, and she would keep it for later, for when it had disappeared inside Rose several times and gleamed pearlescent.

As Sarah slid her hand beneath Rose's skirts, Rose splayed her fan as if to hide her maidenly blushes.

'You'll find something sweet when you taste me,' breathed Rose into Sarah's ear, and fluttered her fan dramatically to hide her wink. 'I put it there for you, not for them.'

It was a tale of temptation and forbidden love, and both Sarah and Rose played it well. And every time they did, Sarah died a little more.

Hannah

Hannah was among the exhibits. The glass cases slept neatly under the arched windows, snug homes for a hundred thousand things in jars. Her little shoes went clack-click on the polished marble floors, and Hannah rejoiced that she had not had to polish those floors; she would not, in fact, polish a floor for the rest of her life; not now that she had been discovered, and proven to be valuable.

She leaned in close to read the labels on the nearest jars: 'chick newly hatched, its abdomen opened', 'genital organ of a doe rabbit on heat', 'clitoris, human'. At the corner of each label was his looping signature: Dr Temple Eustace, Dr Temple Eustace, Dr Temple Eustace. Who knew the name of the doe rabbit or the chick newly hatched? The only name that mattered was the one on the label. She was sure that Dr Temple Eustace would have an adroit and intricate system for organising these specimens but had to confess that she could not understand it. Well, that made sense; he was a man of genius, and she was neither.

She felt a chill on her fingers and realised she had reached out her hand and pressed it to the glass. Before her was 'hand to mid-forearm, human, female', the skin puffy and ivory, the arm looking for all the world as if it was resting beside her own in the audience at the theatre.

Some of the exhibits were taken from Egyptian mummies, which Dr Temple Eustace had himself rescued. He liked to describe it for Hannah: the shaft of white light piercing the desert darkness, the slither of ropes unravelling, brave men dropping down into the ancient underworld. All in the name of empire and the rescue of precious treasures. A tragedy that such stores of gold had been ignored for so long – and, to him, gold was not the shining metal (of which there was plenty in the tombs, which was fortunate as the expeditions were expensive), but instead the black gold of the mummies. It was a most precious of medicines, and Dr Temple Eustace was midway through various experiments to discover why. Others had tried since then to recreate the ancient methods, but none had succeeded in creating a specimen that lasted like the Egyptians. There was so much to learn from these exotic peoples and their curiously immaculate bodies. He described the mummies as a man might describe something holy; his eyes turned far away. She envied them then, those fusty sacks of bones and leather, that they could make the eyes of Dr Temple Eustace turn from this world and see another.

If Hannah was truthful, she failed to see their appeal. Even if she imagined herself dropping down into that ancient hole, gleaming golden in that shaft of foreign sun, sliding off a heavy stone lid and uncovering a body black, hard and shiny as obsidian – still she could not find excitement in it.

Mummies were simply *everywhere*; people used them for firewood, swallowed small pills of them medicinally, crushed them up to make pigments. Dr Temple Eustace had told her that some artists stopped using 'mummy brown' pigment when they discovered how it was made. He harrumphed at that. Imagine, he said, not eating a sausage simply because you've heard of a pig. And imagine also that pig died millennia ago. Would not eating the pig save it somehow? And where was the concern for the old bones being flooded out of the graves in all Glasgow's cemeteries? Were the bodies of their countrymen somehow less worthy than the ancient corpse of an embalmed foreigner? It was a waste to bury bodies in the first place; better, logically, to grind the bones for fertiliser and use the fat for tallow candles. A little distasteful to use local people, but there were plenty of bodies going to waste out in the colonies. Use what you have, says he. No point wasting a thing. He had personally preserved the brains of a skate, porpoise, lion's cub, great horned owl, dugong and young mulatto.

He had no intention of wasting Hannah, she knew that. Every part of her was treasure to him. She was vital, and she was cherished.

She smiled, leaning in to read the text on a tiny label, 'suckling gland of a monkey', it looked like, but – she was brought up short as suddenly the light shifted and her own face was reflected back at her. She was in the case. Blonde-faced, fur-cheeked, bright green eyes gazing out from the thick golden down. She flinched back and cast her eyes down, then clacked her little shoes across the polished marble to find Dr Temple Eustace.

Julia

In the way of fairy tales, Julia was the youngest sister, and the most beautiful, and had the longest and most golden hair. Therefore it was a true shame, a tragedy even, that barely any of her hair remained. She stifled a sad sigh over it, lingering by the butterfly table, pretending to select something from the tasting platter, but really trying not to scratch. The hair was beginning to prickle on her cheeks. She had shaved it just this morning, but she was so healthful that it grew back at a ferocious pace. The pregnancy was not helping; her body, excited to grow these strange new parts, seemed to be growing every part of Julia faster too.

Julia was a wife now, and soon to be a mother, and like all respectable women she removed all her hair. For many years, growing up motherless, Julia thought that respectable women simply had no hair at all. It was only after she and her sisters began their business that she began to see other women intimately, and understood the natural state of the body. It was true that Julia and her sisters still had significantly more hair than the other women, but the difference was not quite so stark as she had believed.

Delicately she selected a pearl-handled tasting pin and pricked it into the nearest morsel: a monarch butterfly, its wings an oily reflective blue. She let it sit in her mouth so that the wings could begin to dissolve on her tongue. She didn't particularly enjoy the wings; they tasted dusty and gritty to her, but she was trying to appreciate them, since they were the most delicate and healthful choice for a woman. She smiled vaguely and let her eyes skim across the room, searching for Feodore. The women fluttering around with their delicate mouthfuls of butterfly, bellies padded round to mimic gravidity, their breasts pushed up, their bare heads gleaming soft in the candlelight. All their parts so round and so pale, like a cluster of pearls in silk. The men all in red, roaring at one another's humour, gnawing on skewers of roasted penis, fists holding hearts still so raw they dripped blood down the wrists of their suits. Julia supposed that was why they were red; not to save the washerwomen's work, but so that even if they hadn't feasted yet, it would appear –

A deep, booming clang sounded from outside. No one paid it any mind, too used to its regularity, but Julia still found it a shock each time. Through the window she watched the looming white moon of the Queen's face turn back and forth, back and forth, as she scanned the city. Her enormous tin arm lifted and banged her gong again on the bell of her skirts. Motherly, she watched over everyone, from the poet in his garret to the mouse in her gutter. Julia had spent most of her life behind curtains, so the enormous tin Queen was still a novelty to her.

Julia feared she would never feel used to the world that Feodore had brought her into. Its startling extravagance. The pomp, the peccadilloes, the panache, the pageantries. She did her best to fit in, but a part of her knew she never would. The same deep-down part of her, perhaps, that itched and pushed out her golden fur, that wanted to drop to all fours and bellow like a beast and push out her child right there beneath the chandelier. How Sarah would applaud her in her full animal glory. So natural. So true.

Julia wondered if Feodore had been to visit Sarah, or even Hannah. Did he still visit the old business? Did he miss Julia as she used to be; the version of her that no one else saw?

'Should you die,' Feodore had said to her the previous evening, as if it was a possibility that she would not, in fact, die, 'I will never take another wife. I will only have mistresses for the rest of my life.'

How Julia's heart leapt at this. No other woman could ever take her place in Feodore's affections. A man can have a mistress and also visit a brothel and also be devoted to his wife. But his wife must have only one lover.

'Mrs Fortune!' called a high, fluttery voice. 'Oh, dear Julia!'

She looked up to see Mrs Eustacia Honeybag and Mrs Hippolyta Fairweather approaching, twin pearls in their ballooning gowns, and she remade her face appropriately. The butterfly had dissolved to grit on her tongue, and she worked her throat painfully until it was gone.

Sarah

Sarah told herself that she was merely hiding behind the wall and watching through the peephole to check on Rose: to check that she was in no danger from her gentleman caller, and also that she was performing her duties to him. The sole reason that Sarah was not lighting a candle was so that the man did not see her. The sole reason she was staying silent was so that the man did not hear her. And the sole reason she was still there, still watching Rose through the peephole, even though the hour had almost fully passed, was that when Hannah was away, Sarah was in charge of the business, and had to keep control of the building and everyone in it.

'How many more?' the man said wonderingly, gazing into the folded pink petals of Rose.

'As many as you wish,' Rose replied airily, which truly was a feat of self-possession, as she was lying on her back with her legs spread wide and her skirts splayed in a bouquet around her.

The man pulled another shining coin from his pocket and pressed it to Rose's labia. The petals parted obligingly, and the coin disappeared.

'That's twenty!' cried the man.

He couldn't see Rose's face, but Sarah could, and so she was the only one who saw Rose's look of exasperation and boredom.

'As I said,' she sighed, 'as many as you wish.'

'Not two at once,' breathed the man. Sarah wondered if he was thinking of the size of his own erect member, and wondering if it had the length – not to mention the weight, girth and heft – of twenty coins. He reached to his pocket, pulled out two coins, and pressed them both to Rose's rose, which swallowed them. He reached again to his pocket, not looking away from the floral vortex, as if mesmerised. His pocket provided no clink of metal.

'That's all I have,' he said, his tone astonished and wheedling.

Rose closed her legs, smoothed down her skirts and stood. She stepped delicately across the room and opened the door. Sarah was sure that she could hear a soft and muffled *clink* as Rose walked. The man, still entranced, joined her in the doorway and accepted her kiss.

'What a wonder you are,' breathed Rose. 'My favourite gentleman, and so generous. I do hope you will return soon.'

The man pressed his hands to his pocket. 'My ... my coins?'

'They are inside me now,' she said, 'and therefore they are mine.'

The man sputtered. 'But that was twenty-two shilling coins! Over two pounds! You're not worth that.'

Rose spread her hands: alas, alas.

'I could have paid a month's coal bill for that! I could have bought a good Sunday suit!'

'And yet you did not. Good day.'

The man hesitated, not wanting to leave – but what was he going to do? Summon a policeman to make a complaint, and consequently have to admit that he had visited the brothel of degenerates and freaks? Little would it matter, as most of the policemen were regular visitors too. The police chief was particularly fond of Eliza, the tattooed lady, who allowed him to prick her with inked needles if he could find a bare patch of skin. It was not the pricking he enjoyed so much as the search.

The man turned and stamped down the stairs. Sarah knew he would be back. A Sunday suit, no matter how good, was no equal to a half-hour of Rose's cunt. The sisters, and Hannah in particular, had worked hard to make this so much more than a viewing gallery of freaks; such a thing could be experienced for a ha'penny, as Sarah well knew, having earned many a ha'penny thus. What the sisters provided was more of a specialist service; for epicureans, connoisseurs, men of unusual taste. This did not mean, however, that they necessarily wished to advertise their presence here.

Sarah stifled a sneeze; it was dusty behind the walls. She thought she'd timed the sneeze to the precise moment that Rose shut the door, but Rose paused, head cocked as if listening. Sarah held her breath. There should be no shame in her keeping an eye on proceedings; it was her place of business, after all. And yet she held her breath, not daring to blink.

Rose smiled and tossed back her hair, as if for an admiring audience. She hitched up her skirts and squatted over a china chamber pot, its inner bowl painted with delicate blooms. With a moan of ecstatic relief, she shat out the coins in a clattering, gleaming stream, so strong that it was a wonder that the china did not shatter, and after the initial deposit, she took a deep breath and released one final coin onto the pile with a delicate *tink*, and she let a few drops of golden piss bless the coins just because she could, and, watching from the dark, Sarah loved her, she loved her, she loved her.

Hannah

Dr Temple Eustace called for the housemaid to add more coal to the fire and waited for it to warm the room further before instructing Hannah to disrobe. All of this was done for the benefit of Hannah herself; she had not mentioned to Dr Temple Eustace that, due to her extra layer, she rarely ever felt cold, though she appreciated these ministrations as she felt it was important that he did not catch a chill.

Presently the room was warm, Hannah's clothes were piled on a chair in the corner, Dr Temple Eustace had ready his notebooks, his magnifier, his torch, his specimen jar.

Hannah took her place on the podium, and Dr Temple Eustace approached, barely able to contain his excitement.

'Such a specimen,' he murmured to himself.

Hannah smiled and closed her eyes. She did not need to look, she preferred to see herself through his gaze. She had been on this podium before, though never in such a bare state as this; today was the first time she would reveal herself to him entirely. She tried not to hold her breath in anticipation of his assessment.

'We begin,' he intoned, 'with the ankle, which is feminine and well turned. The foot is small and shapely, the toes straight and regular, without the knurled skin common in an ape...'

Hannah let her mind wander as he continued. Dr Temple Eustace suffered frequently from ailments, which he attributed to overwork, yet would not lessen his commitments. His work, Hannah knew, *mattered*. It would ensure his legacy and keep his name on the tongues of learned people for many generations. What did the feeble and temporary body matter when you could make a mark for eternity?

'The figure overall is exceedingly good and graceful, with no unpleasantness, and the bosom, hips and waist of a normal woman. Here there is no hint of the baboon, the bear, or the monkey. The face requires elucidation. The nostrils are larger than normal and are distinctly ape-like, as are the lips, which are so large as to appear deformed...'

There was a Lord Eustace in the high medieval period, many generations before Dr Temple Eustace, who was a great landowner; these lands were taken from him when he would not swear fealty to the new king, and after his death his remains were brought to the great hall to stand trial. After he was found guilty, even his bones were burned. Such is the power and pressure of the Eustace name. It was a wonder that Dr Temple Eustace did not crack under the weight of it. Fortunately he was a man of true strength; a man, despite his various inheritances and trusts, who could claim to be truly self-made. Some day he would put his name to the Eustacian Museum of Anatomy. Although the body did not matter, Hannah did wish he would instruct his landlady not to make up his bed while the linen was still damp or to serve him ill-cooked and slovenly suppers; it was havoc on his lungs and stomach.

'The arms are well rounded and pleasantly plump. The palms of the hands are soft and pale, and the thumbs bend normally. At first glance, the pelt of yellow hair on the backs of the hands would suggest a simian ancestry; however, the fingernails are not thickened or blackened, and appear a shell-like pink, of a mostly human appearance...'

There was something, Hannah privately thought, inexplicably spongy about the body of Dr Temple Eustace. He was a flabby,

incurvated person, somehow both rotund and flaccid. His eyes were
damp, his nose constantly ran, and his lips were several shades too
pale. Her sister Sarah referred to him as a 'dollop of slop', but that
showed Sarah's lack of refinement. Her other sister Julia, who had married up and now moved in the most elite society, refrained from
comment entirely, which Hannah took to mean that Dr Temple Eustace was too sublime to be summed up by mere words.

'The labia majora are of regular size, the left slightly larger than the
right, and evenly covered in curly hair of a dark golden hue. The hair
here appears normal for a woman. The labia minora fit inside the labia
majora, and are pink and hairless. The insertion of a pencil into the
vaginal cavity elicits a slight tremor, but nothing further. The smell
and discharge, so far as I can ascertain, are normal. The uterus, felt
through the rectum, seems normal, though undersized. Some medical
men have claimed that hirsuteness is linked to hypersexuality and
bestial desires, but I can see no sign of such depravities...'

Perhaps it was a little cold in the room now; the fire had damped
down, and Dr Temple Eustace had not noticed, so mesmerised was he
by his work. Hannah felt her bosom tingle, her nipples harden. Dr
Temple Eustace brought his magnifier closer, gently lifting a golden
spiral of hair to peer at the curve of her breast.

'This will surely,' he exclaimed, 'be the highlight of the monthly
meeting of the Society for Mental Improvement, Rational Advance-
ment and Intellectual Refinement!' His voice dropped, his notebook
forgotten. He was so close to Hannah that she could smell him: hair
oil, tobacco, burnt wood. She felt a soft pluck, low in her belly. 'A true
medical mystery,' he murmured. 'A wonder.'

Hannah opened her eyes. The examination was over, and it was time
for her to dress. But for ten long, slow breaths, she stood motionless on

the podium as Dr Temple Eustace simply looked at her, and there it was: his eyes, turned far away, gazing as he might upon something holy.

Julia

Since becoming Mrs Feodore Fortune and retiring from her sisters' business, Julia had lived in well-appointed ease at 4 Lochleven Gardens. The family also had a country house, which Julia, if she was honest, found a little stuffy and overfull, out at Rothesay, on the island of Bute. All the chairs were horsehair, and frightfully itchy, and all the windows had draughts. Thankfully they had not had to visit that spring; Feodore's middle brother, Montague, had recently left home in disgrace, in a great deal of debt which he could not and would not pay, and was suffering an alarming fall down the social scale, living very noisily and gaudily in a less-than-reputable part of town, leaving Pater Fortune beset by anxiety and reluctant to show face outside of his city town house.

Feodore and Julia had their own town house, which Feodore had specifically bought because it was bigger than his father's. Again, if Julia was honest – which, of course, she rarely was – she did not find the house entirely satisfactory. She understood Feodore's desire for grandeur, but the two of them did rather rattle around the place, and the housemaids, cook and butler barely counted. Still, soon the baby would arrive, in methods that Julia was not entirely sure about, as while running the business with her sisters she had seen many things go into a woman, but not many coming out. She doubted she had the capacious powers of Rose and did not see how the baby would comfortably exit. If she had not eaten quite so many items from the butterfly platter, might the baby have grown a little less, and so have an easier exit?

Supper was a neat platter of shiny blue beetles, with a small glass of pigblood – not the most ladylike, Julia knew, but Feodore said it was important for the baby, should it turn out to be a boy. She felt fortunate that a tiny glass was all he had prescribed for her; while out walking earlier, she had observed a newly set-up Iron Repository, where a well-dressed man, comfortably seated, drank at the wrist of a young donor. It benefited both to transfer the young blood to the old, as the younger man's blood, Feodore assured her, was 'excellent, but perhaps excessive', but Julia still did not wish to try it. Feodore, being the best of men, had not even suggested it. How it was to be the happy wife of the fondest and most devoted of husbands.

He would be by soon on his nightly visit, but first she had to ready herself. She sharpened her pearl-handled straight razor on its leather strop, which was not necessary as she had done so this morning, but the sound of it pleased her. She called for a basin of hot water and a fresh cake of lavender soap. When it had arrived, she latched the door. She undressed and lathered up the entire front of her body: from the nape of her neck, over the top of her head, down to her face, her throat, her breasts, the stretching globe of her belly; her mons, her thighs, all the way down to her feet. If left wild, the smooth plain of her skin would soon be a curling golden meadow.

As she bent to begin, she caught the scent from between her legs. It seemed to change with each month of the pregnancy. It was good to have a way to mark time with her body, now that her bleeding had stopped. She knew that Feodore missed her menses; every month of their early marriage, she'd expected him to be disappointed when she bled again, as it meant no child was coming; but instead he revelled in the iron-smelling gush of it, enjoying the sight of his member emerging after the marital act, smeared red.

'Blood without pain,' he would murmur to himself as he washed himself off with a damp rag. 'A woman is a wonder indeed.'

She was sure she had mentioned to him that the blood did indeed come with pain: a ratcheting and thudding in her low belly, like an enormous tightening vice. But like all men, Feodore tended to reshape the world, and everyone in it, to suit his vision. She rinsed the razor and patted her skin dry.

Julia was, per Feodore's wishes, a woman of two sides. Now it was time to tend her favourite. From the fireplace she lit all the candles in the room, then positioned them around her largest mirror. She smiled at her bare reflection - then she turned.

The back of her body, from the nape of her neck, down her back and all the way to her heels, was deeply pelted with a spill of golden curls. How they spiralled and tumbled, how they gleamed and winked in the light; the negligent abundance, the impudence, the unreality. With a comb in each hand, Julia groomed herself like the most pampered of house cats. Slowly she slid the comb from the nape of her neck all the way down to the backs of her heels.

She shivered.

She swayed.

She shimmered.

She revelled in the lavish bloom of herself. What a shame that the rest of the world could not see this beauty; could not appreciate the natural and true wonder that was Julia - and Hannah, and Sarah, but Julia most of all, being the youngest and most golden.

Would she go now and wait for Feodore? No, she would not. She would stay here and bask in herself a little longer. It was true that a husband may have many lovers, and a wife may have only one. Only one lover for a woman, she thought, running the comb again from her nape down, down, down to her heels; but perhaps, she thought, perhaps that lover could be herself.

Trussed

Maude gathered while Ottilie watched. The long silk ribbons. The soft strips of muslin. The velvet scarf for her eyes, the silver bell for her ankle, the wooden ball for inside her mouth. And the candles. Of course, the candles: the room must be sensual, intimate, low-lit like a lovers' tryst. More importantly, they both must be able to hide things in the shadows.

The room smelled of wax, polished wood, Maude's skin: to Ottilie, the scents of desire. Maude laid everything out on the velvet-draped table, pausing between each item to place a soft kiss on Ottilie. Ottilie wasn't tied yet, and could reach for the kisses herself. But she didn't want to; she wanted Maude to be in control.

Ottilie's corset was laced tight enough to present her breasts like a gift to be unwrapped, though still lax enough for her to slip things in and out of it. She felt her breath come quick and her head go loose every time Maude came near. After a year of this, their afternoon routine for their nightly work, Maude could still make her mind go empty, turn from plans and logic into feathers and fluff with the simple touch of her hand.

Those hands. Ottilie took a moment to watch them as Maude arranged everything they'd need. The hands pale as milk and strong as iron. Hands that stroked Ottilie to muffled cries every night – and every morning. And perhaps a few times in between.

Ottilie's breath caught as Maude knelt at her feet, holding the silver bell on its fine chain. With a smile, she slid Ottilie's skirt up her calf, over her knee. She could have stopped there, but she didn't. Slowly, she pushed Ottilie's skirt up her thighs, revealing the nothing she wore underneath. Scandalous, they both knew, though how else could she have easy access to the strips of muslin she'd use to mimic ghostly figures in the soft light? But there would be time for that. The bell came first.

Ottilie watched as Maude tied the chain around her bare ankle – another scandal, should anyone see. She took a moment to enjoy the contrast of Maude's skin against hers, the paleness against her own acorn-coloured calf. Next should come the muslin, but Ottilie allowed herself this one demand: she reached out and stopped Maude's hand; moved it instead to the wooden ball, worn smooth as a fingertip, small enough to hold invisibly in her mouth. Maude raised an eyebrow, but followed Ottilie's desire.

Unexpectedly, she slid into Ottilie's lap, shifting up her own skirt to press her bare cunt to Ottilie's own. Ottilie couldn't help letting out a gasp – and that's when Maude slipped the ball inside, following it with a flick of her tongue. This was what Ottilie wanted: to muffle the sounds of what was to come, to be forced into quiet while her body cried out.

The scarf over her eyes, the ribbons on her wrists, the glowing rows of candles: all of this could wait until later. But Ottilie could not. She felt the heat, the steady blood-beat in her cunt.

Maude slipped one hand down to where their bare skin touched. She slid a finger inside herself, then inside Ottilie, who felt a moan build in her throat, held in by the wooden ball.

With her other hand, Maude rolled up the soft muslin, ready to slip inside Ottilie. But she wouldn't do that, not yet. First, Ottilie knew, she would make her come.

The men arrived early. They always did. It wasn't always men – or not all, though mostly – but they were always early. They didn't want to miss a single moment of what was to come. Maude understood; she fell asleep beside Ottilie every night, woke with her every morning, trussed her in silks every evening in between – and still it wasn't enough. She'd stretch the days to twice their length if she could, just to have more of Ottilie.

Maude welcomed in the group of eleven. Plus herself and Maude, this made thirteen – the ideal number for a seance. Her voice was hushed, her head veiled, her back artificially bent to make her look older. All this costuming to make her seem like a venerable widow, or a fallen woman grasping for respectability. She didn't say it out loud; she let her appearance tell the story. It was a role, and she played it well. For Ottilie, they took the opposite approach. Although she was twenty years old, half of Maude's forty years, her hair was left loose and her cheeks scrubbed clean to make her look younger still. Both, for different reasons, seeming to be the type of woman a man can trust. Why else would two women live together, if not mother and daughter?

The men kept their eyes down and their hands tucked in close, nodding courteously as they passed. She seated them at the velvet-draped table where she had made love with Ottilie just an hour before. She wondered if the men could smell them still.

111

The men were the usual mix. Maude ticked off her mental list: the crumpled waistcoats, the ink-smudged thumbs, the shoes high-shined to hide the places they'd worn quite through. She was proud of their establishment, the type of work that she and Ottilie did – but she knew it wasn't what most would call respectable, and neither were the men who came here. One seemed around her own age, his shoulders wide, his calves strong, his hair thick and black. His hands were clean and his shoes weren't too worn; Maude might have been interested, if her heart and mind and body didn't already belong entirely to Ottilie. Still, just for fun, she reached for the man's hand as he passed. He blenched, but didn't pull away; she pressed his clammy hand to her bosom, over her heart, and murmured something about the spirits, the lost loved ones, the insight and sensitivity she knows he possesses.

As he bumbled off, cheeks aflame, Ottilie caught Maude's eye and gave her a chiding look. Maude winked back. Why shouldn't she have some fun with them? Work and play don't have to be opposites, as Ottilie well knew.

With all the men seated, Maude locked the door theatrically and glanced around to make sure everything was in place. The room was lit by the buttery glow of candles – just enough to make Ottilie's skin glow, but not enough to vanquish the shadows beneath the table. She knew Ottilie had the wooden ball in her mouth, the bell around her ankle, the muslin in her cunt – which, Maude liked to think, was still throbbing. The ribbons and scarf were strewn on the table like a lover's discarded undergarments.

Maude approached. The show was about to begin.

Ottilie tried to keep herself steady – though she did allow her breaths to shallow and quicken, just to make her breasts swell above her corset.

She sat neatly at the table, unspeaking, unmoving, trying to keep her props silent.

She let her mind wander as Maude ran though her usual speech. Oh the spirits, oh their power, gentlemen, heed the dangers, we must remember not to get too close to Miss Ottilie, we must not touch her or speak directly to her, we must be respectful as it costs her ever so much to make this contact with the other realm and even if she swoons we must stay back, and so on and so on.

Well, if Ottilie was going to swoon, she'd have done it an hour ago when Maude was between her legs. She felt her cunt pulse at the thought of it; after the men left, she'd let Maude come to her again and take her right there on the table. Perhaps she'd use the ribbons on Maude this time: bind her wrists to the table legs, fasten the scarf around her eyes, and sit right on her face.

The tone of Maude's voice changed, and Ottilie tried to focus. She could feel the eyes of the men upon her. She's never said to Maude, but she likes it. She likes that the men see her bound, moaning, voice raised to the heights of ecstasy and possession and yet they cannot touch her. She's thought about what it might be like to allow one or more of the men to stay after the seance, to watch what she and Maude do with one another. She never would, of course - she and Maude may skirt the bounds of respectability with their work, but this is no bawdy-house. More importantly, she belongs only to Maude, and intends to keep it that way.

With reverential steps, Maude approached Ottilie, then lifted the velvet scarf and fastened it over her eyes. Immediately, Ottilie's other senses heightened: she could smell the sweet-musk scent from Maude's skin, hear the throaty breathing of the gathered men and the shifting of their feet beneath the table. She arched her back a little, allowing her breasts to rise and her throat to stretch enticingly. She kept her hands palm up on the chair arms, allowing Maude to bind her wrists with the black silk ribbons – though of course, one of the hands was a false prop, a model made of wax, and her real left hand was tucked to her side.

She ran through the show in her mind: she would fall silent as the spirits approached, swaying against her bonds. She would shake her leg so that the little bell rang; she would knock her knee against the underside of the table: one knock for yes, two knocks for no. As she was overtaken, she would pant, she would sigh, she would gasp and shriek and moan. With her hidden hand she would pull the long, soft strips of muslin from inside herself and fling them to float down like sinister ghosts in the low light. In the commotion, she would let her head drop down so her hair concealed her face, and then she would spit the wooden ball from her mouth and let it thud-thud-thud across the wooden floor.

Such manifestations! Such wonders! Such uncontrolled power in one so young and innocent!

And was it a genuine attempt for these men to contact their loved ones? Or was it just an excuse to watch a pretty little thing writhe against the bondage of silk ribbons and cry out as if possessed? Ottilie didn't care. All that mattered was that they came here, and that they paid, and that she got to carry on living her life as she wanted with Maude. And if she'd grown to like the feel of strangers' eyes upon her, if she got to reach a genuine climax as she pulled the muslin from her cunt, if she got to enjoy Maude's strong hands trussing her up and unfastening her and slipping into every hidden place – well, she does enjoy her work.

*

TRUSSED

Afterwards, in the privacy of their bed, Maude wrapped her arms around Ottilie. The room was black as the night outside, and no one could see into their top-floor window, so there was no need to close the drapes. The full moon shone on their bare skin, lighting the contrasting tones to the same silvery gleam.

There were no props here. No audience. Nothing to prepare for, nothing to plan, no roles to perform.

Maude reached out and rapped her knuckles on the wall. One knock: yes.

Ottilie smiled. Languidly, eyes closed, she reached for Maude's nipple. She sucked it into her mouth, rubbing her lips against the hardening nub. Maude gasped, and Ottilie slipped her thumb into Maude's mouth. She could feel the heat from her cunt – from both their cunts – and she slid her body up Maude's, their mouths meeting. She could taste herself on Maude's tongue.

This was it. This was all she needed, in this life and in whatever came after: the knowledge that they could bind one another, and not be hurt.

She could go again. They both could. But they didn't need to. For now she could sleep, and when she woke Maude would be there with her. They have tomorrow, and tomorrow, and tomorrow. They could be together now – and who knows? Perhaps it's true what they say about spirits. Perhaps they would be together then too.

2

The rule was: dead girls only. You've got to have rules, you know? You've got to draw the line somewhere, and Mallory and Orla drew it at the dead. It was weird enough, doing what they did; no need to imitate some woman they might bump into at the supermarket or the coffee-shop queue. Not that she'd know. But they'd know. Plus there was always the potential that they were assisting a stalker, or there'd be some kind of criminal case, or they'd get sued. But dead girls - they're fair game. You can't defame the dead.

Orla and Mallory got to the house first: a detached Victorian, chopped into flats sometime in the 1970s. The one they were viewing seemed to have the original frontage, wide bay windows and *Rosebud* picked out in curling letters over the door. The black thorns of roses twined between the letters, and the gold paint was faded.

'Do you think it was called Rosebud originally?'

'I guess so,' replied Mallory, rubbing a thumb over the tarnished brass doorknob.

'Do you think rosebud also meant arsehole then?'

Mallory laughed, then covered her mouth with her hand. 'Orla, come on. Show some respect.'

'To my rosebud? Or theirs?'

They smelled the estate agent before they saw him. He must spend a good chunk of his commission on aftershave, the amount he'd get through.

'So who's Cameron and who's Lee?' he asked, extending a hand that, Mallory could see without touching, would feel damp and overly soft.

'We're the Cameron-Lees,' she said, shaking the hand anyway. 'Ms Cameron-Lee. Both of us.'

'Let me guess. Sisters?'

'Guess again.'

He smiled indulgently. 'You just look so young to be mother and daughter.'

Orla barked out a laugh, and Mallory, who was after all two

months older, took the opportunity to pat Orla on the head. 'We do, don't we?'

Orla added: 'Reckon we could charge extra if we were?'

The estate agent had already stopped listening, and was unlocking the door.

Of course they took the flat. It had lesbian energy. Or if it didn't before, it soon did when Orla ate Mallory's cunt out on the kitchen counter. At certain points, Mallory was sure she could hear a single knock coming from somewhere in the house. The pipes, maybe. When she came, she was loud enough to drown it all out.

'Now you,' she said, when her legs had steadied, patting the counter beside her.

'I'm good,' said Orla. 'Not really feeling it today, you know? I want to fix that curtain pole.'

'Hot,' said Mallory, pulling her jeans back on. Despite her post-orgasmic chill, she knew Orla was right. The sooner they got the flat sorted, the sooner they could get back to work. The second bedroom was going to be the filming room. There was enough space for four different set-ups. In the old place they'd only had two, tucked in the corner of their living room: the standard set-up, as generic as possible, silky sheets and a plain wall; and a teen girl's bedroom, basically a rip-off of a Britney Spears photo shoot, puffy pink bedspread, stuffed bunnies and candy-coloured undies like something you could tear off a cheerleader, the same one these guys never got to fuck when they were fifteen. They'd initially thought they might be doing Britney Spears, but there had been zero requests. Not just for Britney; for celebrities in general.

Most men wanted their ex-girlfriends. They didn't say as much, but the photos they supplied were screengrabbed from social media, and the phrasing examples were one-sided text messages.

So they'd shifted focus. Now they did deepfakes. Dead girls only. They didn't actually check on this, but it was in the T&Cs on their website, so it wasn't on them if the guys ignored it. All they needed was some photos - video if possible - and a loose script of what they wanted the girl to say. There was a possible cast of two: Mallory, almost six feet tall and built like a Viking maiden, long blonde hair, milk-white skin and an enormous rack; Orla, petite and small-boned, deep bronze skin with a dark urchin haircut. Two women couldn't possibly encompass the entirety of female appearance, but with digital tweaking, the right mannerisms, and a customer who sees what he wants to see, it was good enough.

Mallory made more doing this than she ever had working in tech, which was still a rancid boys' club, and Orla had never really settled to anything in particular. Mostly the guys didn't even want porn. Mallory spent a lot less time putting items into herself than she'd anticipated. They wanted a girl they could never have, in underwear or PJs or some girly dress, saying 'oh honey, come here, I love you, I want to hold you, I never should have left you, you're the best man in the world, you're the only man I need, oh honey, I love you, oh honey'. It was kind of sad, actually. Was Mallory the only person in these men's lives who said *I love you?*

But she couldn't let herself get weepy about it. She ripped the tape off a box marked 'KITCHEN?', wondering what exactly Orla meant by the question mark.

Orla's bedtime kiss tasted of dust. Mallory's toes were cold. They had a mattress on the floor and a duvet cover, but they hadn't unearthed the pillows or sheets. The uncurtained window glowed yellow from the street lights.

Orla twined her fingers through Mallory's, watching the moving shadow on the wall. Mallory made sentences in her mouth, then swallowed them without speaking. Orla already knew it all. Her schedule for tomorrow, what she planned to do in the videos. What she would make for dinner at the weekend. Where she wanted to take Orla and what they'd do when they got there. What she hated, what she missed.

'I'm going to sleep,' said Orla, peppering soft kisses behind Mallory's ear. 'I'll miss you.'

'Miss you too,' echoed Mallory.

'Still love me?' asked Orla.

'Still love you.'

She pressed a kiss to the top of Orla's head. They lay back-to-back in the pale light.

It was true: she did love Orla. Of course she did. Orla was funny and hot and creative. She was also impulsive and easily distracted and, sometimes, a little shallow. Her favourite band was the Foo Fighters. She'd seen every *Mission: Impossible* film. She loved macadamia nuts. Was that really enough? Could that really be it forever?

But then Mallory knew she wasn't enough either. She was loyal but pedantic, loving but nitpicky, generous but self-absorbed. She wasn't even a full person, and yet she was meant to be Orla's best friend and lover and confidante and life-organiser and make a home with her and build a career with her and be gentle and patient but also not be a doormat and be spontaneous but also dependable and be mature but not boring and how was one person meant to be everything? What was she meant to do when they were having an argument and Orla was upset but Mallory was upset too; who got to cry and who had to comfort? And what was Orla meant to do when she wanted to go to a sex club and Mallory wanted to have a weed gummy and watch old crime shows? What if neither of them wanted to shop around for the best home insurance deal? What if no one wanted to unload the dishwasher, ever, for the rest of her life? What if they both had things they needed to say out loud, but could never let each other know? Yet they were supposed to lie beside one another every night, knowing everything and nothing about one another.

Orla waited until Mallory's breathing deepened into sleep, then scrolled through an online dating app on her phone. She never messaged anyone; she was only catalogue shopping.

And sure, she'd thought about fucking other people. She didn't want to. She knew if she was fucking someone else then she'd just be thinking about Mallory. But also she didn't want to just fuck Mallory for the rest of her life. Mallory is everything to her, but realistically, how the fuck can one person be everything?

But that's what she agreed to when they got married, and she doesn't regret that. She knew marriage was just heteropatriarchal bullshit designed to trap women, that they were literally *given away* from their fathers to their husbands, traded like sacks of corn. So why shouldn't they take this hetero institution and queer it right the fuck up?

But were they actually queering it, though? Or were they just living the standard cishet marriage-and-mortgage life, with the difference being that the only penis in the house was a strap-on?

Orla meant what she'd said that day. She did want to love Mallory forever.

But, shit. Forever was hard.

*

It happened when they were both being other women.

Mallory was in a pink Juicy Couture tracksuit with diamanté bunnies on the arse-cheeks – the customer's request, what the fuck is *wrong* with men, honestly – and arranging toppings on a pizza while making teasing comments about how much she fancied sausage tonight; later, on the computer, she'd tweak her accent to be more Home Counties, tweak her tits smaller and her arse bigger, tweak her lips wider and hair darker.

Orla was lying on her front on a bed, playing a zombie-killing PlayStation game in lilac cotton underwear, holding the controller as if she'd never seen it before and squealing about how he was so much better at it than her, which of course was total bullshit as she was a fucking machine on the PlayStation, and in fact could be a professional gamer but didn't fancy getting called a whore and a bitch on her headset every time she won; later Mallory wouldn't have to do much at all, Orla was good at accents and already looked a lot like the reference photos, just needed a wider forehead and narrower chin.

'I feel ...' said Orla, and Mallory, hearing the change in her tone, was instantly alert. This wasn't part of the performance.

'Ottilie?' said Mallory, and why had she said that, what the fuck was Ottilie, was she having a stroke, what was she even –

'Maude,' said Orla, 'oh, Maude,' and she rolled off the bed and threw aside the controller, the zombie-killing game still yammering away in the background, and she came to Mallory and sat on the counter, right on the pizza, which actually Mallory had been planning to heat for their lunch after they'd done the videos, she'd got some burrata and hot honey, she'd done a rocket salad, she was going to use that nice garlic sea salt, and Orla kissed Mallory and Ottilie kissed

Maude and Orla kissed Maude and Ottilie kissed Mallory and 'I missed you,' she said, 'I missed you so much,' and they kissed and they kissed and they kissed.

Afterwards, in the privacy of their bed, Mallory wrapped her arms around Orla. The room was black as the night outside, and no one could see into their top-floor window, so there was no need to close the drapes. The street light shone on their bare skin, lighting the contrasting tones to the same golden gleam.

It was just the two of them.

For now.

'Fuck,' said Orla.

'I know,' replied Mallory, but of course she didn't know. She didn't know anything at all.

All she knew was that whatever was happening, it was happening to both of them.

Or – all of them.

Mallory reached out and rapped her knuckles on the bed frame.

'One knock for yes,' she said. Orla looked at her for a long moment, then knocked the mattress once.

So this is how it was. They'd bought a house, and with it had come something else. Someone else. Mallory didn't believe in ghosts. She didn't, she didn't, she absolutely didn't. But –

'Fuck,' said Mallory.

Orla reached for her phone and deleted the dating app. 'I was only ever looking.'

'I know. It's okay.'

A solution they never imagined to a problem they couldn't admit they had.

They twined their fingers together in the cold gold light.

How familiar those hands were. How strange.

'Still love me?' asked Orla.

'Still love you,' replied Mallory, in a voice that was both hers and not hers.

Fangirls

T here's a man inside your house.

  The man has no face.

  The man has a name –

But it keeps changing.

It's just you and him and the deep dark woods.

You could put on the light.

You could leave the house.

You could call someone.

But you don't.

You close your eyes and you make the shape of him in your mind.

You wait for him to fill it.

This is what you have to do –

If you want to see him.

If you want it enough.

And you do.

Oh, you do.

Rosalie, the Fiancée

Once upon a time, a girl fell in love with a boy. That's the story, right? The story everyone wants? That's what they told me to want. I like to do what I'm told.

I first saw him on the TV news. There had been a manhunt. That's what every woman is on, right? That's what we joke about over Cosmopolitans, which at the bar here is just cranberry and triple vodka, but we order them because that's what they drink on *Sex and the City*, and at least it comes in a triangle glass. A man hunt. We hunt with our tits and our lips, save the final kill for our pussies.

He was hot as fuck, sorry about it. Tall, strong-jawed, cheeks scooped out like young Johnny Depp. This black tumble of curls that fell over his dark eyes. Later they'd say that his teeth were rotting out of his mouth, that he didn't wash in prison because he didn't want a knife in his ass and so he stank. Later still I'd find out that was true, but every man is a project, isn't he? Mouthwash helps.

Sitting there in the bar, Cosmo glass sweating in my hand, my girlfriends' laughter already getting loose, the bar stool squeaking under my miniskirted ass, thinking why the hell have they got the news channel on, they should be showing a ball game, or an old black-and-white movie to make the place feel classier than it was, or a nature documentary, lions stalking gazelles, if the manager had a sense of humour, which she did not. Then he appeared, and all I could do was stare up at the TV. I wondered if this is how the Virgin Mary felt when the angel appeared to her. I swear I could hear a hallelujah chorus.

On-screen he was in dirty janitor's overalls, wrists cuffed, top lip in a snarl. He knew exactly where the camera was, and he followed it with his gaze, looking right at me. His eyes arrowed straight into me. The news ticker tape described all the things he was accused of doing. I don't pretend I didn't know. I imagined him in a classic Hollywood pose, taking my face in his hand, the palm calloused from all the things he's held down, pressed along my cheekbone. I'd sigh prettily and lean in. The tip of his thumb would push against my eye socket. My vision would burst into colours. I'd smell the blood caught under his thumbnail.

I thought of all the women he'd been with; the estranged wife who, the ticker tape said, was the reason he'd been caught. On that squeaky bar stool in a room smelling of beer and sex, I saw my future unspooling. All I needed in this world was his dark heart beating beside me in bed. It had beat beside his wife and she'd pretended she didn't hear it, pretended she didn't know. But he wouldn't have to pretend with me.

I never went back to that bar. I didn't need to hunt any more. I'm waiting out his sentence, just as he is, and every time I lie with him in that conjugal room with its polyester sheets and wicker basket of condoms, I hear his heart beat against mine and all I think is: I knew, I knew, I knew right from that first sight.

I know exactly who he is: the key that will unlock my most hidden parts. With him, I can be everything I want to be.

Bella, the Fan

I'm him. Not exactly *him*, but *like* him. No, screw that: *better* than him.

Because he's old, and he's in prison, which does sound kind of badass but actually I bet it smells of man farts and cheap cleaning fluid. Not unlike shop class at school. But more rapey.

My name is x_Jack_x_Switchblade_x. Cool, right? I mean, a little lame too, but I made the account two years ago and I can't change it now. Anyways the girls like it. We play, me and the girls. Just online.

There's nothing wrong with it. We're reading and writing, we're using our imaginations, we're working on our empathy skills. We should be able to present this shit as homework.

I'm the boy they want and can't have – but online, all I want in the world is them. They know exactly who I am, what I've done, and I quirk a smile at them and say: *hey. I see you* and it's the best thing they've ever heard because no one, fucking no one in their lives, actually sees them, and I talk to them like they're the only person in the world.

Some girls have romantic saviour complexes. They know a boy is just a boy, that he's soft as a marshmallow underneath and all he needs is a little love and understanding.

Sure, there are beasts – but all he needs is a beauty. He'll see that true beauty in her, no matter how deep it's hidden. Because he's so *deep*, so *dark*, a misunderstood outcast, and they feel like outcasts too, so he's the perfect boy to find solidarity with. All she needs to do is save him, and he'll save her right back.

Some girls don't want to save him. Asshole to the world, but good to his girl. Choke me, Daddy, I'm your princess. They think they'd be the exception – that everyone else would be killed, but the boy would see something special in her, would recognise right from the first glance that she is not like the others.

They'll go on a glorious murder spree together like the Joker and Harley Quinn, go out in a hail of bullets like Bonnie and Clyde, die for love like Romeo and Juliet. Maybe if they got caught they'd cry that he'd forced her, manipulated her – but that would be bullshit. It was a willing desire.

For a while I thought that was funny, these totally standard girls, just like all the others, why would a killer think they were special? Like why wouldn't theirs be the head in the fucking jar or the corpse raped until she rotted apart?

But then I figured it out.

Some girls, *that's what they want.*

They want to be the head in the jar.

You can't talk, can't move, can't get older, can't make the wrong choice, can't be too frigid or too slutty – just held, forever, at the moment of your most desirable, when someone wanted you so much that they'd kill for you. Imagine being so special, so precious, that the individual parts of you are worth saving.

A girl is at her most desirable when she stays young, doesn't speak, stays nice and still so she can be looked at. What else are teenage girls told, except that they're the most beautiful when they're dead?

All girls want a murder boyfriend.

And he's the perfect one.

We've all seen him on the news and the true crime sites and the social media rabbit holes. Those eyes, that hair, that smirk. Say what you want about him, but if he was less murdery he could've been on some teen drama show. It's easy to fit into his skin.

I know exactly who he is: a manic pixie nightmare boy.

He's the teen girl dream, so I can be too.

Claudette, the Ex-Wife

On my sixteenth birthday, no one paid attention to me. Including me. Everyone's eyes were on the TV, where the news reported that another girl's body had been found. Her name is as emotive to me as my own: Gabby Villeneuve. She was taken the week after her sixteenth birthday. She was a saint. If she wasn't in life, she became one after she died. Beautiful, generous, high-achieving. Perfect in every way. It made sense that the killer would choose her. Anyone would choose her.

But every time I thought about Gabby Villeneuve, I couldn't see her clearly, because a shadow fell across her face. The shadow of her killer.

I could already see him in my mind. He was strong, sexual, unswerving. He was virile; a lady's man. His hair was thick and fell over his eyes. His lips were soft. His body was brawny and sinewy, like a welterweight boxer. He was cruel when people weren't good enough. But that was okay, because I knew I could be good enough.

There are so many things you can be haunted by. When I was a little girl, I often imagined a winged black horse taking me away through the night. I think I'd heard someone say 'nightmare', and I knew a mare was a horse, so it made sense to me that nightmare meant a horse that came for you in the night. I told him that once. We were lying in bed, in that honeymoon time when you spend a lot of time in bed, and you love to put things in one another's mouths, and every word that comes out of those mouths is surprising and magical to you. I told him about the horse, and I laughed a little, because I felt nervous and kind of silly, and I don't know if I wanted him to laugh too. But he didn't. He turned to me and sat up on his elbow with his chin in his hand and he looked right into my eyes – that was the thing with him, he could look at you like he was the only person in the world who truly saw you, and later I wondered if he looked at them like that, all those women, if that was the last thing they ever saw, and I think as last things go it's not such a bad one, to be truly seen like that. He took me seriously. I don't think men realise how much women need that. To be heard, and seen, and understood. He always did that. I'm not saying he was always good to women, but you can't say he ignored us.

In return, he told me that when he was a little boy, he imagined unearthing a woman in the forest, finding her like treasure. I asked him if he'd got that from his mother reading him fairy tales, if he was thinking of Snow White in her glass coffin, or Sleeping Beauty woken with a kiss. I imagined him unearthing me from the darkness and the silence, of gazing at me in wonder and saying: *oh my love, my precious thing. Were you waiting for me all that time?* And I would say to him: *yes, yes.* He turned away from me then and said men didn't have time for fairy tales. But I know that's not true. If there was ever a fairy tale he knew inside out, it's *Beauty and the Beast.* If neither of us had ever heard that story . . . if, if, if.

He didn't kill Gabby Villeneuve. They never found who did that. But I often wonder, if not for her, and all the time I spent thinking about her - and more importantly, the man who chose her - would I have let him choose me?

I know exactly who he is: the beast from the fairy tale. But no matter how good I am, he will never change.

Beauty, the Prison Guard

It's hard for a woman to be known for something she's done. Mostly women aren't remembered for anything at all, and if we do know their names it's that they're the wife or daughter or discarded fuck-toy of a more accomplished and famous man. They can ride on his coat-tails, but then they're stuck behind him, trying to pretend he's not farting in their faces.

There's one more way for a woman to be known. She can be murdered by a famous man. The more elaborately, the better. Suzie Barbot.

131

Jean Beaumont. Marie Prince. Gabby Villeneuve. Names we all know, and why? Because of him. The Pig King, so-called because parts of his victims were fed to ... well, let's just say it wasn't a king. They never caught him. The faceless, ever-shifting man who haunted all our girl-hoods. Would he come for us next? What would we do if he did? And did it even matter what we did, or said, or wanted, or were?

A lot of people think he's the Pig King, but it was never proven. The only one he was convicted for, in the end, was the wife. Not even proven, and still he's famous for it. Who do you know that's affected so many people's lives as him? People he's never even met know his name, but he doesn't know theirs. He doesn't have to because they don't matter. Why does he get to matter? Why does he get to matter, and I don't?

I had so much potential, you know that? I was always top of my class in school. Graduated early. Studied psychology. I was going to be a criminal psychologist. Then I had to quit because they changed the terms of my scholarship. I applied for a correctional officer job, just temporarily. I thought – I have no idea why – that it might help me to move into my chosen field. I might not be strictly qualified to work with the inmates in a psychological capacity. But surely it would help, I thought. The more experience, the better. That was twelve years ago. And here I am. Here I fucking am.

And there he is. Known. Named. Seen. The primal terrors of sounds in the night, sharp knives and dark alleys, your own flesh turned to meat – distilled into a human being, a real live man, a horror with a heartbeat.

I think the most frightening thing about him is the nothingness. Not the shallow affect of the psychopath, and not the banality-of-evil ordinariness. It's that there is simply nothing there. I have hours – *hours* – of recorded conversations with him, and let me tell you, he is one of the most tedious men I have ever met. The self-aggrandising, the victim complex, the circular logic, the repetition of the same tired old anecdotes. He holds back details of the murders like an eight-year-old with a secret den. I meet everything he says with wide-eyed absorption and he's like a leaky tap, drip drip drip.

For a while the other inmates were calling him the Professor because he hung out at the library so much. He read all the law books he could get his hands on. He's got this plan that he's going to mount his own defence. This is all just so perfect, I couldn't have planned it. I joined in, called him the Professor too. He's an idiot, of course, or he wouldn't have got caught; but I don't want him thinking that. I want him thinking he's smarter than everyone in here, including – especially – me. If he thinks I have the intelligence of a sponge, he'll let me soak up everything I need.

I join in when they call me Beauty, too. I know it's a joke. My looks were never my strength. But I prefer it that way. Everyone's looks fade in the end, and I've seen what happens to women who rely on them too much. I've got something better than looks. I've got him.

My love is hard fact. It can be counted and measured. 343 newspaper clippings, 15 videos, 29 conversations recorded on my Dictaphone. A testament of devotion. Not devotion to him; God no. Devotion to myself, of who I should have been. Who I will be, because of him.

I know exactly who he is: the way to make my name mean something. And I won't even have to die.

Bella, the Fan

We live in a nice place. My parents are comfortable and mostly ignore me. I've never been woken by gunshots or mugged in the twilight. The only violence here is the silent kind that happens behind every locked door and inside every girl.

Once I found a jar of baby teeth in my parents' room, but I swear there were too many to be just mine. I wondered if they were my mother's from when she was a kid.

Or I had a sibling a ways back who died or left. My parents are older so it's possible.

It could be a serial killer's trophies, for all I know. Wouldn't that be a trip!

If I was alone with you, I type, *I wouldn't be able to hold myself back. I would have to be restrained.* In response, a tongue emoji. I knew she'd like that.

I think it's true what they say, that he's the Pig King. That means he'd already killed someone before I was born. Weird to think that. He'd lived a whole life before mine even started.

I could have known him when I was a kid. He could have been my uncle. He could have been my creepy neighbour. He could have been my babysitter's boyfriend. He could have stuck his big hand down my little pink pyjamas when she was out of the room. He could have squeezed a soapy sponge over my little puss when I was in the bath. He could have looked at my tiny mouth and thought: yes.

He didn't, obviously. No one paid me that kind of attention when I was a kid.

I want you to lock yourself in the bathroom, I type, *and wait for me to come for you. And while you wait, you can come for me.* Fire emoji, peach emoji, fire emoji.

The day I was born, the police were doing a fingertip search of the fields at the edge of town because Gabby Villeneuve had just been found. There were another three but she's the main character.

She was the youngest and the prettiest, and she'd never done anything. The others, the papers said they were sex workers or they'd had a bunch of boyfriends. They'd been out late at night – but Gabby was snatched outside the library where she'd been staying late to do homework. She literally couldn't be more perfect. I bet she had half a Best Friends heart keychain on her backpack.

I will never let anyone else have you, I type. *You are mine, body and soul, forever. I will take you by force if I have to.*

She's past emojis now, just key smashing, *akskskdkfjansnf.*

When I was little, we learned about the Vikings in school, and then we played at raping and pillaging all summer. We'd heard the word 'rapier' and we thought that's what it was. Cutting stuff up with a long swishy sword.

I sign off with an eggplant emoji and a tongue emoji. I think she's already gone. She doesn't like to digitally snuggle.

I don't want to *be* a man. Or. I don't know. Do I? I want to have what men have. Not a dick necessarily but the rest of it. Though a dick would be okay.

I think I just want to be someone else. And if I have to be him – that's better than being myself.

He's a suit that I wear, and you know what? I'll outgrow him. But that's okay – there are a million guys out there, and most of them are just scaffolding anyway.

I'll find another hollow man, and make him real.

Claudette, the Ex-Wife

He didn't kill me. He's in prison for killing me, except I didn't die. I think, for him, that's the worst part.

He used to call me his doll. It's funny that we think dolls are for little girls, when it's what most men want. A life-size plaything, tender and tentative, graceful and girlish. Four poseable limbs and a wide, wide smile. Little girls love their dolls, but that's nothing to how he loved me.

Real love, real deep down to the bone love, love right in the guts and the marrow of a person – that kind of love *hurts*. Why wouldn't it? What's the point of anything if you don't really feel it? If it doesn't dig its claws deep, you could just shake it off and walk away.

But not my man. He'll never walk away from me. Every morning when he opens his eyes and sees the underside of his cellmate's bunk, he'll think of why he's there. I'll be his first and last thought, every single day.

Here's what the therapists always say: what's the difference between a man who beats his wife and one who kills her? One got angrier. They only say that because they don't know him. He never did anything out of anger. It was so much more than that. I don't think anyone will ever understand him the way that I did.

It's not his fault that he couldn't change. But what it's taken me a long time to realise is that it's also not my fault that I couldn't change him. That's the thing about a beast. If you love him enough, he'll change. Oh, he didn't change? Then you didn't love him enough. But no one ever loved the way that we did. He was a fairy tale, abrupt and bloody, teaching me a lesson I never quite learned.

I remember when I knew how much I meant to him. We were watching something on TV, I don't know what, it doesn't matter. He wasn't looking at the TV, though. He was looking at me. He did that a lot. I swear I could feel his eyes on me even when he wasn't in the room.

I know what you're thinking, he said. I knew what I was meant to reply, which was *sorry*. That was the easiest rule to remember: he always knew, and I was always sorry. But I didn't. I looked back at him, and I said: *no, you don't*.

A hard look came over his face then, his eyes flat and empty. For a second, he wasn't a person. I felt something rise up in me like a wave. It wasn't fear. It wasn't desire. It was both. I felt my heart start to canter.

He came to me, so slow and so soft. That's how I know it wasn't anger.

It lasted a long time and I had passed out by the end of it. His hands were around my throat, slick with blood, and I heard the cantering thud of my heart like hoofbeats and the winged black horse was finally coming for me.

I remembered then about that woman he wanted to unearth in the wood. Such devotion he showed her, such care. Don't we all want to be that woman? Don't we all want to be found? I fantasised about the discovery of my body. It would be some other girl's sixteenth birthday but no one would pay attention to her because everyone's eyes would be on the TV, talking about my body. I imagined a cop, close to retirement, determined to make his final case a good one. Or a rookie, thick-haired and serious-eyed, trying to make his name. Solving my murder would be the last, or first, good thing he would do. He would avenge me.

But I didn't die. I woke to blue lights and the judder of a stretcher sliding into an ambulance and at the trial I testified from behind a screen and so the last time I ever saw him was that final moment before I lost consciousness, when he tightened his grip on my throat and looked right into my eyes and he saw me, he truly saw me.

Beauty, the Prison Guard

Before this, I worked in a women's prison. It's crazy to me that some people still think that women aren't inherently violent. That every incarcerated woman is just a naive, blushing nun who got caught up with a bad man.

My own mother left me in a dumpster when I was a day old. I still had my umbilical cord. She took the time to arrange the garbage bags on top of me, to hide me. Lucky for me the guy from the pizza place sneaked a smoke in the alley and heard my muffled crying. Tell me that's not violent. Tell me she didn't want me to die.

The same act can be considered violent or not violent depending on the circumstances under which it's done. Think about war. Think about saints. Violence has no fixed reality. The only reason we don't think women are violent is due to the concept of what we consider violent. A fistfight is violent, a gang shooting is violent. A woman smothering her newborn, overdosing her sickly mother, drowning her kids because her new lover doesn't want them – that's not violent, that's just sad.

There are a lot of baby-killers in women's prisons. Sexual abusers too. The 'other woman' kills the lover who won't leave his wife; the wife kills her husband for his money; the nurse kills her patients because she feels like it. But sure, all women are naturally gentle nurturers. Poor little lambs, so easily led astray by a man. She was forced, she was provoked, she's mentally ill. You can't blame them, can you? As if half the world's population never feels rage, greed or spite.

I used to think that women read romance novels for the same reason that men read true crime. Wish fulfilment. It lets them think: that could be me. It's not, but one day it could be. One day I could fulfil my most secret desires – fucking, killing – and I'll get through this day by dreaming of that one. But then I started noticing how many women read true crime. My theory still holds.

Women write him love letters, can you believe that? They send him nude photos and their worn underwear. The mail censor tries to take those, obviously, but I do my best to make sure they get to him. I know it's best to keep these women at a distance, so of course I don't. I want him distracted. I want him high on himself.

I think the most frightening thing about these women is the opposite of what I found in him. These women are something. They've got lives, homes, families, careers. They're not walking around with obvious voids in their lives. A lot of them are professionals. Highly intelligent. Doctors, lawyers. Psychologists, even. You'd think they'd know better. But sometimes it seems like the more you learn, the dumber you get.

The guys here, some of them never sat in a classroom in their lives. But they are smart. In the ways it matters in here. Crafty, organised, impossible to bullshit. That's what's great about him. He thinks he's better than these guys, so he doesn't learn from them. If he was smart, he'd learn from the women in prison. When men want to escape, they dig tunnels and climb over barbed wire. Women, they enlist others to help. But he's relying on the last person who's actually going to help him: himself.

I know exactly where I'm going to be: in a stage, lit by studio lights, giving TV interviews about him. For certain high-profile cases, I could be an expert witness in court. I've been thinking about titles for my first book. *Close to a Killer*? *The Intimacy of Evil*? I'll keep working on it.

He thinks he's pure desire, unrestrained, an animal, and he's right.

But what he doesn't know is that I'm the lion tamer. And at the end of the day, the lion goes back into its cage, and the tamer goes wherever the fuck they want.

Rosalie, the Fiancée

There's a TV movie about him. They had to change his name and some details about him so that he wouldn't sue, because he was never actually convicted of all those murders. The actor playing him is hotter than him, but in a bland way. I masturbate to that movie sometimes. Sit there with my hands down my pants, watching him. I'm not usually so garish, but it does give me a giggle. That's the story, isn't it? The boy does things while the girl watches. Masculine dominance, feminine submission. Misogyny can be a gift, if you let it be. Small equals helpless. Powerless equals innocent.

Everything about me is a costume, and I'm clever about it. The demure dresses. The soft makeup. The job as a middle-school teacher. The voluntary work. Who cares if it's real? I look innocent, and that's what matters. It's all about the story.

I like to do what I'm told. The trick is to only be told to do what you secretly wanted all along. They told me to get a man, so I did. They told me to let him drive, so I did. Whoever he's going to mow down on the way – well, that's not my fault. I'll say I was only a passenger. And let's not pretend I'm the only one. Take a minute to think about the number of movies and books about a young woman getting involved with a man despite the fact (because of the fact) she suspects he killed his previous wife.

I used to have this fantasy. Beauty and the Beast. I'm hardly the first woman to have a Disney sexual awakening, but mine was different. I was so bummed out when the Beast turned into a human prince.

Beauty loved him as a Beast, right? So why would she then want some-one entirely different?

Fuck the prince. I want the Beast. I want a man of muscle and fur, a man with blood in his teeth. I'd clamber up on his broad back, a huge sword in each hand, and we'd rampage our way through the world. Seems pretty clear to me that's what Beauty wanted.

He's not going to be inside forever. He didn't even kill her, and they didn't convict on the others. All I need to do is wait it out. I've got far enough with my own pretty ways, but now I need him. I want his simplicity, his honesty. I want a fist in a face, a bullet in a brain. I want to do things his way. And if we get caught, I won't even have to protest innocence. I can sit and weep into my hands and the story will be told for me.

It doesn't matter who he is, not really. What matters is who I can make him into.

He won't be a man any more. He'll be a gun with my finger on the trigger.

Linger

The best part of the day. The early-evening light was buttery, and the bus in its cocoon of fogged windows slowly wove through the quiet streets, the untrimmed trees scraping like fingernails on the roof, everything bleak and damp, and waiting for her at home, hot tea and a wedge of cake she'd saved from yesterday, only a little stale, and the last scrape of margarine too, the old stove filling the kitchen with warmth, and out the back the comforting squeaks and flaps of a family of bats. She'd run out of eggs and the only milk was powdered, but it would be fine enough in tea. She didn't bother to cook when it was just for herself.

The bus window lit the bombed-out houses, shadowed cavities in the mouth of the streets. The reconstructions had been going on for almost a year, but it was slow work, and the farther you got outside the centre, the poorer the area, the more gaps remained. Nettie still spent her days diligently sorting the letters, because working at the post office was her job and her job was important to her, but she did wonder how many of them were addressed to a pile of rubble. There had been a huge backlog of post during the war, which was only now beginning to un-gum. How many of the letters' senders were nothing more than ghosts? How many of the recipients? Everything seemed so bright now after the years of blackout, the town lit up like fairyland, the cinema marquees and cafe windows and street lights all bright enough to dazzle; though sometimes the new light only served to cast the shadows deeper.

Things had changed in Nettie and Tom's marriage, and she liked their new routines. She still did all the housework, but only what she deemed vital. She no longer blackleaded the grate. All that labouring with the stiff brush, the tube of Zebrite – what would be the point? By the following morning it would be ruined from Tom sliding all over it, smuts and smears spread to all corners of the house. He was always most active in the dark. Now that Nettie thought about it, there had been little point in blackleading the grate even when she was a single girl. Was her purity really defined by how dark she could get her fire? Was she less proper, less worthy, if a patch of tarnish gleamed through? She was so busy with her job, and her voluntary work, and looking after herself, that sometimes there was only a semblance, a soupçon, left over for her husband.

She turned up her coat collar and hunched her shoulders against the damp chill of the bus. She hoped the parlour would heat up quickly and chase the cold from her bones. She was still on coal, because it was cheaper than electric. It would be all fine and good if she could afford a maid to clean out and lay the grate, and more importantly to be careful enough not to get coal smuts on her elbows and thighs the way that Nettie does. Mrs Tanner, Tom's mother, had a maid, so Tom is used to much higher standards of cleanliness than Nettie. He's used to a higher standard of everything, Nettie suspects, but he doesn't complain about it. He doesn't complain about anything. Not any more.

Nettie wondered where she would find Tom when she got home. It had become rather a fun mystery for her to figure out. He was somewhere different every day, and he never gave her clues. It was their little game. He could be under the bed, perhaps, or under the couch. Dozing in the stockings she'd hung to drip-dry over the bathtub? Twisted in the curve of the hot tap? She hoped he would stay hidden, and then emerge only when she thought she was finally alone, when she was freshly scrubbed and in her nightgown, slipping tentatively between the chill of the sheets, only to see that the shadows in the corner of the ceiling were not shadows but were, in fact, Tom.

She had not planned for this thing with Tom. Nettie Lightbody was quite happy with her life, thank you. Yes, there was a war on, and it had been going on forever, and every day the newspaper's requiem for the dead got longer, and it was all very sad and horrible. But rationing didn't bother Nettie; she wasn't particularly fussed about food, and this gave her an excuse not to make elaborate meals. The blackout could be a bore, but the dark town made the stars bright and clear, layer upon layer, in a way that Nettie had never seen before. She'd been able to start working, sorting letters at the post office; a position that wouldn't have been available to her before all the men shipped off. She was busy at the Women's Voluntary Service every Wednesday, handing out cups of tea amid the air-raid debris, looking rather fetching in her green uniform. She'd even started hand-to-hand combat training at the WVS. She couldn't see herself thrashing a German, exactly, but it couldn't do any harm. The enemy wasn't the only danger on the blackout streets; she knew plenty of women who'd been accosted and didn't even see the man's face. When houses were bombed, there was plenty that didn't get destroyed, and Nettie had outfitted her house very finely through salvage. Her social life was more active than ever, since so many establishments had closed due to shortages: she put on bridge evenings, staged plays, hosted poetry evenings, organised musical concerts. On Saturdays she simply turned up the radio and had a few friends over to dance and drink. Night after night was filled with music and laughter. Nettie was having a jolly old war.

Of course, her house might be bombed and blast her to pieces in her sleep, but then one could get hit by a bus or drop dead of a heart attack, so really what was the difference?

She was still alive.

She was not mourning anyone in particular.

And it was perfectly possible to have a party in the dark.

But here was the problem: everyone. Oh, how they *talked*. The foreign spies had nothing on Nettie's neighbours. There was so little to do on those endless blackout nights, and even the tiniest blink of light from the opposite window was enough to spark a new piece of gossip. Mrs Veal wears red lace. Mr Valdemar keeps odd hours. Mrs Jessel had her baby only six months after Mr Jessel came back from duty. Miss Lightbody keeps company with various doubtful people.

The situation was becoming tedious. Nettie was the only one left of her family after her mother died, so she had inherited the house, and saw no problem with living there alone. But she knew what people thought about a single woman. What was the point of keeping a house if a man wasn't coming home to it? The last few times she'd tried to use her ration coupons for treacle and sausages, Mr Van Tassel at the shop had told her they'd run out. He said they'd run out of gin, too. She knew it was a lie. It would be so much easier if she could be married – or even better, engaged – but then there would have to be a man around. There were so few men left, for a start, and while they might be fine for a night or a weekend, after that they grew tedious. Nettie had eyes and ears, and she'd seen perfectly well what a marriage was. Cleaning, cooking, lying back and thinking of England, listening to a man grumble on and on and on. Shaking out doormats and polishing door handles. No thank you.

Nettie's neighbour to the left was old Mr Umney, who seemed to be at the kitchen window no matter what time Nettie passed, his hands in the sink, peering round the net curtains. Nettie had been throwing her milk bottle tops and chicken bones in the rubbish rather than keeping them for salvage, because honestly it had come as a surprise to her that bones could be used to make soap and milk bottle tops to make fighter planes, and she was a little dubious about the whole thing. Mr Umney was probably thrilled to think that his saucepan or his shilling were part of a bomber. But it seemed to Nettie that sorting the cereal boxes into one pile and the ripped wellington boots into another was just a way to keep everyone busy. Turn off your lights, grub around in your own remnants, and don't ask any questions. Mr Umney had acquired some rabbits, which he intended to use for meat and to sell to a furrier. That, however, was months ago, and the rabbits had not reduced in number. Nettie suspected that Mr Umney had made the fatal error of giving the rabbits names, and now couldn't bring himself to kill them. She understood, in a way; every time she passed his garden, she bent over the fence and stroked the rabbits' soft ears. How sweet it was, the way their little noses twitched. She imagined Mr Umney was telling himself he *liked* mock-turtle soup, actually, and wouldn't prefer a rabbit pie after all, and really wasn't it better for the war effort to keep the rabbits alive for something or other, to turn into a tank or make toasty little hats for the boys on the front line.

Her neighbours to the right were the Tanners. Mrs Tanner, her three horrible daughters Kitty, Bunny and Lily, and the golden boy Tom, who had enlisted on the very first day of the war and hadn't returned since. He sent weekly letters to the female Tanners, which Nettie knew because she sorted them. There was something solid and filling about Tom; he was a thick slice of brown bread, a dense meat pie, a brown-black pint of Guinness. He was just the sort of man to be a husband.

One drizzly Sunday, while Nettie drank tea uncomfortably in her mother's armchair, wishing the horsehair stuffing wasn't quite so horse-like, a wail came through the front window. Not an air-raid siren, but Mrs Tanner, with a telegram in her hand and an awkward-looking man on her doorstep. Well, thought Nettie. That'll be the end of Tom.

And that's when it came to her. She didn't have to be a single woman. She didn't even have to be a fiancée, or a wife. She could be the best thing of all: a widow.

It wasn't difficult to be Tom's ventriloquist. She'd opened many of his letters before, just out of curiosity, so at first she simply mimicked his shallow and simplistic tone. But Nettie's Tom grew better with each missive. He was brave and strong, glad to be fighting the good fight; but also how he wished that war didn't exist, and everyone could just stop fighting. He understood that Prime Minister Churchill was holding things together; but also wouldn't it be so much better for people to share resources in a more socialist way? Women should have more freedoms. The poor should not suffer so. Most of all, how he missed his darling Nettie, and how he longed to be home with her. He promised to seek out an unexploded bomb so that he could liberate its green silk parachute for Nettie to make into an evening gown for one of their many parties. He only hoped that she was keeping busy with her work, and her volunteering, and keeping her friends close, so that she wouldn't miss him too terribly.

It really was too sad about all those dead boys. Nettie could feel the ongoing war turn her mind to gloom a little more each day. Yes, there was still dancing, and parties, and drinks, and friends, and men. But it was all starting to ring hollow. You'd go out and have a dance and share a joke with a stranger and the next day he'd ship out and never come home. She didn't know how to feel about the haunting intimacy of knowing that the last human touch that Arthur or Ernest or Peter or John ever had, before their plane plummeted from the sky and burst into flames, burning them right to the bones, was her own.

When she had a decent enough stack of letters from Tom, all back-dated appropriately with stamps from her work, she knocked on Mrs Tanner's door.

'We were keeping it a surprise,' Nettie said, a single tear rolling cinematically down her cheek, 'so we could tell you together when he got back.'

Mrs Tanner stared silently at the letters, as if they were about to explode in her hands, but Kitty appeared from behind her.

'When he got back! And now he ... now he ... he never will!' She dropped to her knees and wailed. Nettie was a little irritated that Kitty had out-dramatised her, but Mrs Tanner swept Nettie into her arms, cooing 'My daughter, my daughter', and so thrilled was she that the plan had been a hit, it was all she could do to keep looking forlorn. Nettie rather felt she was a great example of wartime pragmatism. She had outfitted her home from things that dead people no longer needed. She was alive, and she needed things. Tom, now, was a thing that no one needed – except her.

Nettie found, to her delight, that being wife to a dead man was the perfect situation. Mr Van Tassel always had a bottle of gin and a tin of treacle set aside for her, but of course she was already owned by another man, so he wouldn't be expecting a fumble for it in the back room. Mr Umney still peered through his net curtains at her, but nodded respectfully and kept his gaze strictly neck-up. She could have people round whenever she wished, because there was certainly no funny business now; they were simply helping her to cope with her tragic loss.

The only downside was that she had to go for tea at the Tanners' every week, to reminisce about Tom and eat fish-paste sandwiches, meaning that her thoughts of poor Tom now smelled rather odious. Her technique was to stay docile and demure, nodding along with whatever Mrs and Misses Tanner said. Over the months, they seemed to forget that Nettie was even there. She did feel she was doing a rather kind public service, for the war had languished into a fifth year, and the mood everywhere was gloomy. Young love was always a balm for the soul.

Mrs Tanner poured the tea, and Bunny sighed and stretched out her feet so that everyone could see how she wore actual stockings, not gravy-painted legs, and not even laddered or saggy-kneed. She must, thought Nettie, be gadding about with an American.

'I rather feel this war has gone on forever,' she said.

'The previous one didn't,' replied her mother, 'and neither shall this one. Now, Kitty, dear, do be generous with the jam. There's plenty more. I always make two batches, just as the Dig for Victory leaflet says. One for quick use, and one for keeping.'

'I think it's useful to have so many heavy glass jars,' said Lily. 'Should a German break in.'

'How oddly your mind works, Lily,' said Mrs Tanner.

'As if you could kill a German with a jam jar,' scoffed Bunny. 'You can barely stomach the red sinews in the chicken.'

'If I got a chance,' retorted Lily, 'I would kill a German with a jam jar. I'd rip out his eyes and stamp on his heart. I'd kill him with my bare hands if I had to. I'd burn their hearts but they haven't got 'em.'

The grandfather clock's ticking seemed to echo as the room fell silent.

'The Germans are just people,' said Mrs Tanner lightly. 'People just like us.'

'They're not like us!' said Lily. 'They killed Tom! They'd kill us too!'

'And you've just said you'd kill them,' spoke up Kitty, gesticulating with her jam-smeared knife. 'So they really are just like us. And besides –' here she pointed her knife at Lily's delicate little hands, barely meeting around her teacup – 'you'd barely be able to throttle a mouse with those.'

'It's what Tom would have wanted,' said Lily sulkily.

'Tom was a pacifist,' said Nettie.

'He most certainly was not!' Mrs Tanner burst out.

Bunny laughed, the same high tone as the china cup tinking onto her saucer. 'He enlisted to bash the Bosch. He said so himself. I'm sure he took plenty out before they got him.'

Nettie bit her lip, burning with indignation. Bunny's version of Tom was no more true than Nettie's. Why did she get to be the authority on him? Nettie was the one who loved him. Nettie was the one who had exchanged dozens of long letters with him. They were engaged, practically married; surely his confidences to his fiancée were more valid than whatever throwaway confessions he might have given his middle sister?

She never visited the Tanners' again, because the next night it was bombed. Nettie, not yet in bed, sitting by the dark window at the tail end of a party, less than an hour after the last guest had left, consumed by a vague malaise, watched as the sky lit up in fireworks and the Tanner house collapsed like one of her cakes, the soft fruit of the Tanners inside squashed to nothing. Her own house, a miracle, juddering like a jelly but left whole.

The next day, there was a thin and dirty ice over everything. Shattered glass glittered in the ruins. The street held the acrid reek of the bomb and a mean stink of gas from the broken pipes. Somewhere, a tap dripped.

And that would have been it.

But then the war ended, and Tom came back.

The bell rang early. Nettie, somewhat hungover but not enough to stop her going to work, opened the door to a ghost.

'Hello,' said Tom Tanner. There was something wrong with his mouth. It twisted to the side, caught up in a mass of scar tissue that spread like a slap across his cheek. 'I don't quite know...' he swallowed, and it sounded painful. 'I don't quite know where to go. My house...'

He motioned to the hole in the ground where the Tanner house used to be.

'The Tanners,' said Nettie, wishing her head didn't throb quite so much. 'They're dead.'

'All of them?'

'Well,' she said. 'Not you.'

They stared at one another for ten long seconds before Nettie remembered her manners – one really should invite one's fake fiancé, whose entire family and home had been destroyed, inside. It was too late to hide the gramophone and easy chair she'd salvaged from the Tanner house; she'd just have to hope Tom didn't recognise them. While picking through the wreckage, she'd felt a surge of fear when she peeped into the cellar and saw it was splattered red; the bodies of Mrs Tanner and Kitty and Bunny and Lily had been taken away in an ambulance, she'd seen it happen; but then she realised it was not blood but jam. Mrs Tanner and her batches of jam 'for keeping'.

For a moment she'd felt like giving up. Throwing herself down into that filthy, jammy cellar and never getting up again, letting herself starve while weeping over the shards of Mrs Tanner's plans.

But what good would that do? So she'd dragged the easy chair back to her house, where Tom now sat.

The wedding was exactly as one would expect. Tom was indeed just the sort of man to be a husband. When they kissed, he held both her hands in his, softly rubbing her wrists with his thumb. It was winter, and he wore leather gloves, their tips singed soft from lighting cigarettes. Later, in the dark, she thrilled to hear him toe off his shoes and unbuckle his belt. He smelled of tobacco and bread.

They had ice cream at Mildmay's, lunch at Van Tassel, and a film of Nettie's choice, the content of which Tom never had an opinion about, though he always sat quite happily and watched. Once they got an orange, and shared it piece by piece, the juice so sweet and sharp that Nettie almost gagged on it.

The fishmonger greeted her as *dear Mrs Tanner*, and gave her the pick of the strange new imported fish: megrim, saithe, witch sole. They all looked repulsive to Nettie, and she couldn't be faddled to cook them anyway, but she did appreciate the nepotism. A few times she bought the witch sole, then fed it to abandoned cats on the way home. But good times, like war, can't last forever.

Nettie was not her usual buoyant self when she got in that evening. There had been a peacetime celebration in the square, but it had a desultory air. The streets were mucky with slush, the texture of black pudding. A few bedraggled girls hung on their soldiers' arms, damp with drizzle, red lips pulled into a grin. People milled about, setting off fireworks, dancing on top of air-raid shelters, climbing on statues and yelling aimlessly. The whole thing made Nettie feel thoroughly depressed.

She arrived home to the worst sort of Tom.

'We've been married over a month,' he said. 'And it's time you stopped working.'

'Hello to you too,' Nettie replied, shaking the rain off her coat and hanging it on the peg.

'You must look after your husband and children.'

'We don't have children.'

'What will everyone say about you, married and working? That I can't afford to keep you! I forbid it.'

'Tom, darling,' she said. 'You *can't* afford to keep me. And you're on to plums if you think you can forbid me from doing anything. My answer is no.'

But of course, he could. He owned her, body, mind and soul. He could lock her in or out of the house. He had a legal right to her body in whatever way he chose to use it. And he was not pleased with anything Nettie chose to do.

Nettie would have been happy to just eat some stale bread with margarine and Smedley peas – no time wasted over the stove, so you could get on with something else. She'd even be fine on asparagus or kidney soup, which came in tins, kept for months and was not rationed. A small supper and a draught of nerve tonic before bed, and Nettie was content. But Tom wanted meat, meat, meat. And meat needed time and attention and the reading of many women's magazines to find ration-friendly recipes. Nettie Lightbody had not been a woman who spent her time clipping out recipes, and Nettie Tanner wouldn't be one either. She served him a tin of soup and some crispbreads, then went off to get on with her hand-to-hand combat training. But Tom made his protest known. Heart, tongue, sheep's head, trotters, chitterlings: you can, he claimed, get any of them from the butcher without ration coupons. Look, right here, he'd clipped a few recipes himself from *Woman* magazine, for sheep's head roll and brains on toast.

'If you wish to make sheep's head roll,' said Nettie, buttoning up her coat, 'then do feel free. I shan't need any, thank you.' But of course, she ended up making the sheep's head roll, and actually it would have tasted fine if her mouth wasn't bitter with resentment.

Next, she didn't use enough dolly blue when washing the whites. There was the wrong sort of white, you see, and also the right white; and the way Nettie liked them, not a startling, blinding white but ivory, like the thick lid on fresh cream, was no good at all. What will everyone say about their creamy, unstarched sheets? The colour of semen and floppy as Tom's cock? His mother used Fuller's earth and bran for her cretonnes and fur, ammonia-ed all her bloodstains before anyone even saw them, why couldn't she, why couldn't Nettie, why couldn't she be exactly like his mother except instead of pushing Tom out of her vagina she let him put his cock in it?

Tom slept in the Morrison shelter, which Nettie had only put in the bedroom so that it would be out of the way for parties. One wasn't meant to sleep in it. She shuddered at the thought. Like sleeping in a coffin. All he wanted to do in the evenings now was stop in and stare into the fire.

If Nettie did insist on him coming out with her, he would act so morose and rude that she became embarrassed and left. If she went out without him, she'd come in to find him standing in the dark between the windows, back flat against the wall, arms at his sides, an expectant look on his face.

'The flying glass!' he whispered. 'It can be deadly.'

'Why are you going to break the glass?'

'Not me! The Germans. A bomb. I heard the sirens.'

'There were no sirens, Tom,' replied Nettie with a sigh. 'And what on earth is this?' She turned the strange metal object over in her hands. Potato masher? Testicle clamp?

'Self-locating bomb remover,' called Tom from the other room, still flat against the wall. 'You attach it to a broom handle and it swivels and grips the bomb to disengage it. The best part is that you can operate it with one hand, leaving the other hand free for a protective shield.'

'A protective shield,' said Nettie. 'For an incendiary bomb. Your hand.'

But it didn't matter what she said, because Tom had stuffed cotton in his ears, as well as a piece of rubber in his mouth to protect him from impact. Nettie didn't speak for the rest of the evening. She realised that she'd happily never speak to Tom again in her life.

Nettie missed the Tom from her letters. Perhaps it was their youth that had made them so light-hearted and idealistic. Their early courtship was imbued with the glow of deep promise and whimsical adventure.

She did not want to admit it, but the Tom she loved had never existed. The quiet, content, idealistic man who wanted Nettie to live her life and be happy: he was dead and gone, a ghost, a figment. That wasn't Tom.

This was Tom. A needy child. A constantly emptying stomach. An employer who would never promote her. A bomb that could go off at any second and take her down too. The war was over, but not in this house.

Nettie still cooked all the food, such as it was. There was a type of poison that tasted of nothing.

They had rats, she'd say if anyone asked. But they never did.

As Nettie stepped off the bus she glanced up at the sky, but there was nothing to see. The streets were brighter than before the war, everything lit up in desperate celebration. The moon was still discernible, but not a single star.

To the right of Nettie's house, the hole that was the Tanner house remained. To the left was Mr Umney's, its intact windows dark. She bent over his fence and tangled her hands in a dozen soft rabbit ears. Mr Umney had died, she didn't know of what, and his house was still empty, but the rabbits remained. They'd chewed through the mesh of their hutch and taken over the garden, doubling in number over and over until the grass was barely visible beneath the heaving, hopping mass. Nettie reached into her bag and tore several leaves off a cabbage, tossing them into the garden. Then she heaved the whole thing like a rugby ball, enjoying the empty feeling when it left her hand. It would mean a smaller dinner for the next few nights, but she didn't mind. Cabbage made her fart anyway.

She unlocked her door and went into the house, closing the door on all hurting things. She glanced around for Tom, but couldn't see his shape in the shadows. Perhaps he was in the drainpipes, or curled around a light bulb. He liked those liminal spaces. Landings, corners, top shelves.

She put on a pot of soup to heat, the kitchen lit by a single striving lamp. Nettie wasn't one to reflect, but in that moment she did. She'd kept on her post office job, but her other activities had rather fallen by the wayside. The camaraderie of the WVS had faltered, and instead of something fulfilling and exciting, it now seemed to Nettie nothing more than a haggery of housewives who talked only of the best ways to boil up a pudding, and the wild abandon with which their neighbours squandered butter. With no bombed-out ruins from which to serve tea, her green uniform just felt silly. Every task felt like busy-work. As the years receded, Nettie felt herself recede with them.

But, she thought, perhaps that's no bad thing. She realised that she'd settled, after all, into domesticity. But she found she didn't mind it. Companionship was a boon, and there was a lot to be said for the familiar rhythms of marriage. At times she missed the bright flutter of her butterfly friends, but she found she preferred the dark and slow-beating moth wings of Tom's company. It had been hard to love Tom when he was alive. But she loved his ghost so very, very much.

She went to the window and lifted the curtain. Let the soup boil over. It doesn't matter. Soon Tom would come out from wherever he was hiding, and they would have a lovely quiet evening together. Look at the town, lit up like a fairyland. It's nice that the lights are on now. Though one does rather miss the stars.

Sucker

From the moment I saw them, I was obsessed. It was like someone had switched off the light, but suddenly I could see in the dark.

At first I thought they were mother and son. He looked like an Italian model from the 90s, black curls and scooped-out cheekbones and a jaw like the edge of a shelf. She was preserved in the way that rich older women are, silver-blonde hair resting on the big fur collar of her coat.

They were moving into the house opposite, which had been stripped to the bones by the previous owner, who intended to flip it for profit but died of a brain aneurysm before he got the chance. We live in a row of large terraced sandstone houses with faux-Gothic flourishes: turrets, weathervanes, windows with hundreds of tiny panes. The houses used to be split up into poverty flats, a whole family in a single room, all working long shifts at the steelworks, even the children. Then gentrification, and each house expanded, carving bits out of other homes, stealing individual rooms and then swallowing up entire families. Each house now loomed, spider-like, grasping.

I'd been working from home since the pandemic and spent most of

my workday in the bay window on the first floor. I should say work-
nights; I was a night watchman for a museum. You might not think
that's the sort of thing you can do from home, but it turns out they
prefer it: every square foot of the place is covered with cameras, so I
can see everything at once, and this way there's no danger I'll be
injured by an intruder and sue. All have to do is raise the correct
alarms if there's a fire or a break-in. I have money, the sort of inherited
wealth people tend not to admit to, which is how I've got this house.
But being middle-middle class doesn't get you as far as it used to. I
didn't need *this* job, but I needed *a* job, and this one was as good as
any. I lived alone and silent, as if asleep. I ate when I felt hungry, slept
when I felt tired. There was nothing and no one to arrange my time
around, so I lived outside time.

I'd tucked my desk at the window so I'd have my back to the room;
as well as my office it was the spare room, and since I didn't have any
friends and my family didn't speak to me, it had become a graveyard
of flattened cardboard boxes and things I never got around to return-
ing to shops. Rather than confront the detritus of my life, I chose to
look outwards: at them.

They didn't have curtains, so I could see right into their rooms. At
first I thought it was all temporary, since they were just moving in, but
as the weeks went by and nothing changed, I realised it was a choice.
Their house was like a movie set: great swathes of white muslin hanging from the ceiling, billowing like clouds; one or two pieces of very
old, very expensive furniture in each room; nothing electrical, nothing modern. They kept odd hours, went out dressed up most nights,
and played a lot of music: as in, they actually physically played it, she
on the piano, he on the violin. I recognised the music; I don't know the

names of classical composers, but they were famous pieces, things I'd heard on adverts and film soundtracks. Even though it was winter, and cold enough to make your teeth hurt, as soon as they started playing I opened my window to hear.

I kept changing my mind about their ages. He could be in his forties but incredibly well preserved, in the way only money can buy; but he had the ease, the insouciance of a man in his early twenties. She was easily sixty, composed and calm, but with a shake in her hands. Her skin was wrinkled and supple like thin paper that had been folded and refolded many times, smoothed over by loving fingers.

And so they made their little world together, and through the glass I watched them. Possessive, controlling mother with her clingy and overachieving son, I thought: but then, one night, when I forgot to put on a light, I saw them lit up like a stage play in their bedroom. He cupped his face in her hands and kissed her mouth. Fervent, possessive. Violent, even. He stroked his hands down her shoulders and she shivered. He took hold of the shoulders of her pale, silky dressing gown and ripped it from her body. Not in a fit of passion, but slowly, deliberately, tearing the fabric to reveal skin just as pale and silky. She didn't touch him but she also didn't stop him; it was as if she was following instructions from a director off-screen.

They were right by the window, and I wondered then: did they *want* me to see? Me, or just anyone? Of course I was curious, but I didn't like feeling like a bit-part in their drama, so to make a point I switched on my light and left the room to go and make dinner - or supper, or breakfast; I didn't know the time or what meal was appropriate, but I only had scrambled eggs and liver anyway so it didn't matter. As I fried the liver in a pan in my dark and stuffy kitchen, the radio burbling in the corner, I thought of their bodies, coming together among the billowing curtain of their stage set, each watching the bright, empty room I had left.

It was around that time that I started to get sick. The details don't matter; I'll just say it wasn't the type of thing that gets better. Once it starts, you can do various things to slow it down, but it just plays out until the end, which is the same end waiting for us all. I suppose no one gets to live outside time, when it comes down to it.

The treatments were unpleasant and tedious. Not painful, but still my body fought against them, shuddering and bilious as if knowing that something was inside my body that shouldn't be. The treatments also took hours, which gave me plenty of time to daydream – nightdream – about how to get invited into their house. Into their lives.

I could steal a parcel from their step and pretend it was delivered to me accidentally. I could bring round a welcome-to-the-neighbourhood basket of pastries and wine. I could fake a heart attack outside their house, so they'd have to rush out and scoop me up in their arms, both of them holding me close, giving me mouth-to-mouth in turn, his cold full lips and her thin soft ones, both of them pulling me back from the brink, wanting nothing more than for me to go on living.

Once, like a child, I knocked on the door and then ran away. I wanted them to come because I had summoned them; for something to happen because I had made it so, even if it was only opening the door. Usually he was so composed, but I must have taken him unawares; I watched from behind a hedge as he stood there, his chest bare, solid and oddly waxy, his black suit trousers hanging low on his hips, his feet bare. He blinked slowly, as if drunk or pulled from a deep sleep. He stood there for far longer than necessary. The night had iced every surface with diamonds and my feet in my boots were numb, but he appeared unaffected. Finally he closed the door, and it was as if nothing had happened, except for inside me.

The treatments continued, to no apparent purpose. They were always scheduled in the early evening, which at that time of year was as dark as midnight. I took to walking there and back, as the judder and stark lighting of the bus nauseated me. I think I had begun to disconnect a little from reality. I wasn't sleeping well, and spent much of my time in darkened rooms, watching the house opposite, touching my fingers to the cold glass of my windows.

The city at night felt like a hospital, bleak and unknowable. The lighting was so bright it washed everything antiseptic. None of the signage made sense and the walkways twisted labyrinthine and every-thing felt plasticky and over-bleached. The bridge across the river had hidden speakers piping out whale song, and in my insomniac detach-ment I found it made perfect sense, that whales would be singing to one another from a silty city river as they navigated sunken shopping trolleys and families of eels.

After the treatment, during which I thought of the hollows of his hips and the soft notebook of her skin, I walked home in silence under a blank sky. Every house on our street had a security light, each of which flashed on as I passed. Mine didn't, and neither did the one opposite, which is why I didn't see him at first.

'A girl like you,' he called over to me, 'shouldn't be out alone.' He was leaning against his front gate, exhaling a thin stream of blue smoke up to the sky, something thin and black between his fingers. Of course he was too fancy for it to be a cigarette. A cigar, maybe? I didn't know exactly what a cigarillo was, but it was probably that.

'Why's that?' I said.

'Because there are men like me about.'

Not threatening, not seductive, not even particularly friendly. Just stating a fact to help me, like pointing out that my shoelace had come untied. I started to cross over towards him, but stopped halfway, in the middle of the road. If a car came round fast, it would hit me. I found I didn't care.

'They'll kill you,' I said, nodding to the cigar.

He laughed at that, much longer and more genuinely than my snippy comment warranted. Even though I'd made the joke, I felt like I was missing it.

All that time I'd spent figuring out how to get close to them, and all I needed to do was walk home alone in the dark.

He mashed out the cigar on the gate so it sparked. He put the stub of it into the bin, opening the black plastic lid and dropping it with a thud, and there was something so prosaic, so deeply ordinary about that act. He was just a man who put things in the bin. He ate food and he shat it out. Sometimes he felt awkward, sometimes his knee twinged, sometimes he got an eye infection.

He winked at me and went back into his house without saying another word. I realised then: there was something so childish about him. A little boy playing dress-up.

And I was worried for him. What was she doing with him, this woman twice or three times his age? What did she want from him?

Perhaps I shouldn't have been surprised that, the following day, he invited me to dinner. He did this with his usual theatrics: a thick, creamy, heavy card put through my letter box, the elaborate letters embossed in gold, 'We would be honoured if . . .'

I went straight across the road to accept. I didn't have embossed golden notecards, so I knocked on their door and waited.

'Yes,' I said when she opened the door. 'I would like to come to dinner. Clair would. That's my name. It wasn't on the notecard so I didn't know if you knew. It's Clair.'

'Eleanor,' she said. 'Eleanor Laluyaux.'

I waited for her to add *call me Ellie, call me Nell* – but she was neither of these. She was an Eleanor. His name I never learned. I know that sounds strange; I spoke to them often, visited their home, inveigled myself into their lives – yet his name never came up. He loomed so large for both me and Eleanor, we never had to refer to him by name. He was the only 'he' we ever spoke about.

But I'm getting ahead of myself.

I don't think it's necessary to narrate every encounter we had. That first dinner was exactly as I expected, a mixture of the surreal (oysters reddened with beetroot, a platter of sweetbreads, tart wine in heavy goblets) and the ordinary (hearing them disagree over the correct method of stacking the dishwasher). It was also the first of many. I continued to observe them, though without the barrier of glass between us in the dark.

They communicated in a way I consistently failed to understand, but envied. Sometimes they spoke in a foreign language, one I didn't recognise. Sometimes it sounded like Italian, sometimes Romanian, sometimes a soft shush like Icelandic or a series of hissing tongue-to-teeth sounds like Catalan. They listened to one another with a deadly seriousness, but then what appeared to be vital information was dismissed with the wave of a hand and a tut against the teeth.

Often there was no language at all. In response to an unvoiced question, he kept his unblinking gaze on her until she inclined her head slightly with a smile. He raised his eyebrows as if acknowledging an answer. It made something in me ache to see the intimacy they shared.

I wanted them; that will be obvious. I wanted her but I didn't want to take her from him. And I wanted him but I didn't want to take him from her. I wanted them both, but not together. I wanted each of them to find me forbidden fruit; to yearn for me in their secret depths, to watch my windows in the night.

I noticed that all the mirrors in the house were hung at his eye level. He checked them often, letting his gaze track as he passed, watching himself in motion. He was at least a foot taller than me or Eleanor, so when I was there I couldn't see myself at all. I hadn't realised how used I was to watching myself as I washed my hands in the bathroom; an opportunity to fluff up my lank hair or pull down the lower lids of my eyes to assess their redness. In their bathroom, all I saw was a blank wall and the reflection of the very top of my head.

As the weeks passed, and I began to miss more and more of my hospital treatments, I found myself pulling away from him and focusing more on her. We spoke often, Eleanor and I. Every time he left the house to do whatever mysterious things that men like him did, she called to me. She did this by sitting in her bay window with a white silk scarf at her throat. I responded by fighting my thorny way through the woods behind the house and forcing open the broken window of their large glass conservatory. We met in a room that I struggle to name: a small nook at the centre of the house, probably meant for storage; it had no windows and was very warm, and we sat there on a dusty chaise in the glow of a hurricane lamp, and she told me her story, piece by piece.

There was no real need for this melodrama; she could have phoned me and I could have crossed the road to her front door. But her story seemed to need these throat-clearing theatricals. Without, it was too real, too horrible.

Here is what she told me.

If I sound nostalgic, said Eleanor, it's not because I was happy in those years. But I feel affection for how I was then. I miss that girl who thought she was in control. Did you know that the term 'nostalgia' derives from the Greek words *nostos* and *algos*? Nostos, return. Algos, pain. Nostalgia is the wound we keep reopening.

When I was a child, everything about me was fine. Grades, average. Friends, average. Looks, average. I was shy and a little silly, I doted on my little brother, every Wednesday I stole a penny candy from the local store. I don't know what it was that set me apart from the other girls. I wish I had known, so I could cut it out of myself.

I met him at the school gates. I assumed he was leaving classes, as I was. We dated a little. My parents were old-fashioned and didn't want me getting too serious, though they never forbade me from seeing him; they only wanted me to focus on my schoolwork, which I already found a struggle, and this was no problem for me, as although I did like dating him, really I was more interested in going to the cinema with my friends and playing on the hockey team. But he grew convinced that my family were keeping us apart.

He told me we were the only two people in the world. He told me he would make it so.

He killed them in the night and left the bodies for me to find. He sat outside my house with the car running and the passenger door open.

You have to understand about obsession. It's not how you feel about a band or a movie star or a distant crush. Real obsession has guts, and it has claws, and it makes you bleed, and it leaves scars. It's not something you can just grow out of or forget about. It has consequences.

In those vaporous days we moved often. When you have no family and no home and no one knows who you are, you're free. Not free like a bird. Free like you can be taken.

I've never had a job or a friend. I've never owned anything. Never slept alone in a room. He makes the world, and I live in it. All I know is what he's told me. All I have is what he's given me. Is that from the Bible? It feels like it's from the Bible.

I want you to look at me now. I want you to look, and to listen carefully to this part. I was thirteen when he took me. Now I'm sixty-eight. But he isn't.

It took a while for him to tell me the truth. He would sometimes say strange things. *I was never a child*, he would say. *I will never grow old. I will never not be this.* I think I knew, deep down, before he told me. If he felt me start to drift from him, he would bind me back.

Once, when he thought I had lingered too long over a map in a rest stop, he took me to the animal shelter and ate all the kittens. He didn't drain them of blood, like you might expect. He unhinged his jaw and ate them whole. Their little bones made his gums bleed, and he liked that.

We saw a flyer for a frat party, and he was so enraged by the thought that I might want to go that he ripped out all their throats. I believe a serial killer was blamed for that one.

I knew for sure what he was the first time he hurt me. I know that sounds ridiculous; as if the deaths of my family didn't hurt. As if I felt nothing for cats or frat boys. But physically, he was always cautious with me, until the day he wasn't.

He hurts me very deeply, but never violently. Very slowly, he gouges and he scratches and he carves. He eats morsels. Then, when he's finished, he feeds me his blood, and I heal without a scratch. I have lived for fifty-five years with a murderer, and there's not a scar on my entire body.

One day you knocked on our door and ran away, do you remember? You hid behind a hedge and I suppose you thought we couldn't see you. But the thing is, he can always see you. He can see in the dark, and even if you're well hidden it doesn't matter because he can read minds. He always knows. It's not possible to hide from him. He's usually so cautious, but that day he opened the door unprepared because he had just finished healing me. He goes tender and dreamy when I drink from him. He becomes drunk, like a glass of water.

How could I be average among all that? Would a girl who was just fine cause a boy to commit mass murder? One girl in a million can push a man that far.

In the early days, he asked me often. He wanted us to stay young together.

But he wants me to come willingly. He will never force me, he says. He'd never force me to do anything. And I suppose he hasn't. He didn't force me to go with him. He hasn't forced me to stay with him. He simply killed everyone who ever cared about me.

I have to hold this one thing back from him. If I choose eternity, then I can only have eternity with him. He will own me forever. And so I get older, and he does not, and every time he asks me I say no, not yet. Not yet.

Saying no to him – saying yes to my inevitable death – is my final act of love.

*

So there it was. Eleanor's story. Of course I thought she was a fantasist, or delusional, or playing some strange mind game with me. But her explanation made as much sense as any other, and if I argued with her then I might not be invited back, and then what was there for me? My darkened rooms and the burble of the radio and the bright-lit stage of their house across the road? Besides, it could be true. I had very little life left anyway, and a lot more to gain than lose.

Over those months, while we sat in the low glow of that room in the belly of the house and Eleanor told me her story, my fascination for them both did not diminish. If anything, it grew. Not in size - it was already insurmountable - but in complexity. My fascination became layered and contradictory. It intensified to a heady, dense, stinking knot at the centre of me, like ambergris in a whale.

Imagine, I thought, being loved like that. Whether Eleanor dies tomorrow or lives her whole life again, whatever she says, whatever she does, she is loved more than most people will ever be. If nothing else in Eleanor's life is true, then she can hold to that one thing: how much he loves her.

But along with that, another realisation: I had disrupted something by coming into their house. I knew that things had changed. I saw it, whether through the window or over the dinner table. I was there, a ghost between them.

I was beginning, by then, to feel a little like a ghost. I often went away. Not to anywhere in particular, or not that I remembered. I had absences. Waiting in queues, walking down the street. I'd completely given up on my treatments by then, and the letters from the hospital had stopped coming. They likely thought I had moved, or died. I suppose I had low blood sugar, or low iron levels. I would just drift away momentarily. I quite liked it. A blurred quiet, a little death.

I rarely saw him alone, but one night I decided to smoke a cigarillo while leaning on my front gate. It pleased me at times to imagine myself as him, and at other times as Eleanor.

It was winter again, and standing there in the dark I realised I still hadn't fixed the security light on my house. I didn't notice him until he was in the middle of the road. He started to cross over towards me but stopped halfway. His eyes were black pits with no reflection.

'I saw you once,' he said. 'You've changed, but I recognised you instantly.'

'Is that meant to be a compliment?' I replied, blowing a long stream of smoke up to the sky. 'You and Eleanor have only been here a few months. I can't have aged out of recognition.'

'You were young. Barely more than a child. I saw your face at a window, just for a moment. I was ashamed to stare, but I couldn't help it. I thought – how beautiful it would be to live here, and never go away again. Years passed, and I still dreamt of you.'

'And that's why you moved back,' I said, and I winked, though he wasn't looking at me, but up at the wispy scuds of evening cloud.

'I had to know,' he said.

I waited for him to answer his own question. I hated when men did that: goaded you into asking what they meant. It was a kind of neediness.

'You're dying,' he said, and although I had known it was true for a long time, it still gave me a jolt to hear it. 'But you don't have to.'

'Everyone dies,' I said, and I must have gone away again, because the next thing I knew he was right beside me.

'Say yes,' he breathed into my ear. A year ago this would have turned my insides pewter and slick, but now I knew too much. I had seen him stack the dishwasher poorly. I knew he took out the bins every fortnight.

'You want me,' I replied. He went to speak, but I wasn't finished. 'You want me to come willingly.'

'Yes,' he said.

'Then yes,' I replied. 'Midnight.'

I knew he would like that, dramatic bitch that he was. In the second before he smiled, a thought came to me. The only way for Eleanor to be safe from him was to be the only one. There it was, the unspoken part of her story; the reason she had told it to me at all. His interest in her was dwindling, and he had fixed on me instead. She'd thought he'd wait forever, but forever is a long time, even if you're immortal. If there was another option, if she really was average, was only fine, was replaceable, then what was keeping her alive?

I shivered for a different reason then, waiting for her to emerge out of the shadows. Waiting to feel her teeth ripping out my throat.

But, I thought later, after he'd flounced off to wherever he went, while I was scrambling eggs in a pot because whatever was going to happen I thought I'd need some protein, he hadn't killed my family. He hadn't kidnapped me and moved me from place to place my entire life. I wasn't thirteen years old. I didn't have to live the story he wrote for me.

Just before midnight, I let myself into the house across the road. It was freezing cold; all the windows were open, making the great swathes of white muslin shiver. The piano, which from my window had seemed elegant and perfectly proportioned, looked different close up. It squatted, gleaming, in the centre of the room like an enormous black beetle. Even with my breath held, I couldn't hear either of them in the house.

Down in the cellar, it didn't take me long to set up. In my own cellar there was a pit, six foot deep, originally used to store potatoes or work on something mechanical or perhaps to murder men, who knows; all that mattered to me was that there was an identical pit in this cellar. My supplies were cheap and easy to arrange. Zip ties, sawdust, tent pegs, a scalpel with a yellow handle, big plastic bases to stop beach umbrellas tipping over on windy days, which I filled with water from the tap. When full, they were heavy, but I managed to push them into position.

'Are you there?' I called up the stairs. A pause, then: 'Please, I need you,' I cooed, scalpel in hand, voice high and soft with an edge of desperation, just the way that men like him liked. He came down the stairs like a wisp of black smoke, but he wasn't smoke, he had a body every bit as solid as mine, and he couldn't see in the dark after all and he couldn't read minds after all because he didn't see it coming, not at all

He was imprisoned easily. Most of his blood spilled out onto the sawdust I'd tipped into the pit, and what little was left in his body meant his movements were tiny and weak, more like twitches than anything intentional. Even if there hadn't been a large wooden tent peg in his mouth, he wouldn't have had the energy to speak. He wasn't quite dead. I was pushing the last of the heavy umbrella bases over the lip of the pit to hold him down when I heard Eleanor gasp beside me.

It was tempting to really nail it home to her; to tell her that he only had power all those years because she believed he did. But it felt a little cruel at this point. Most likely she'd already reached the same conclusion. And it can't be easy for her. She must feel a pull towards him. Those hands that held her down and held her close. Those eyes that watched for her through every night. That voice that told her the story of who she was.

So here's the choice. Make it with me now. Here we are, in that sad little cellar, holding Eleanor's creased, velvety hand, watching him slowly writhe in the pit. There's a smell of old blood and sawdust. No one in the world knows any of you are here. He is nothing now; forget about him. He was only ever a tool, a one-time passcode to be instantly discarded. All that matters is you and Eleanor.

Option 1: She can get him to turn her, then she can turn you, and you can both live together forever. You can live outside time. The soft kiss of snow that never melts. Dreaming on a slow ship from one side of the world to the other. Her gentle fingers on the piano keys, her voice from another room, the dappled sun coming through the trees: trees that you planted as acorns, and watched grow.

Or, option 2: You can walk out of this cellar together, still human, and leave him there, as whatever he is. You can pool the money and time left to you both, and have it be enough, and live every second, every penny. You can grow old together, and die together when you've used up all your time. You can plant acorns and trust that someone else will enjoy the tree when it grows. You can both go together.

Or you can both stay together.

SUCKER

Or.

There is another option.

You, leaning on the gate, exhaling a thin stream
of blue smoke up to the sky.

You're better at being him than he ever was.

You can own her just like he did.

What a neat space he's carved out and left empty.

You can fill it, and more. You're outside with the car running

and the passenger door open.

Devotion

it is all ways summer at the sanctuary –

or at least that is how it feels to me then –

summer bewitching my body –

low gold sun in my eyes & sweetshit scent of the cows in my nose & pollenblow catch in my throat –

i am new at the sanctuary & i dont know any thing yet –

though even when i am not new father fleck still says i do not know any thing but that is a different matter –

because i dont know any thing i cant be trusted with any thing –

so when its my turn to catch the fish we go together –

not me & father fleck obviously he is too busy with holy things good pure important holy things too busy to do actual work like catching fish & bringing in cows & picking peas & plucking chickens & baking bread & sweeping floors & making candles & collecting honey etcetera –

that is work for girls to make them holier –

father fleck & other men being already holy i suppose –

there at the sanctuary the girls are me & jennet issobel beatrice

matilda agnes gilleis lizabet petronella jehan hanna isidore oh &
euphemia thats every one i think –

but the only one who matters to me is –

the only one is –

actually i think i dont want to say her name –

the feel of her name in my mouth is –

it is –

i am sorry –

i can say a lot of things –

but even now that i can not say –

i can not tell you about her but i can tell you about the fish –

& how it is that day with the line & the string & the hook & the
worms –

watching her bait the hook with the sad worm writhing & twisting
its body saying no no no –

& i know that is silly & fanciful & i know that worms dont say any
thing so i also dont say any thing –

i just put my worm on my hook –

& think about how some thing must suffer so that another thing
can have comfort –

we sit there on the bank the grass is sweet & soft around us –

the feel of her beside me is sweet & soft also –

the sun hot on our heads the birds singing prayers the world laid
out so nice just for us –

& i would gladly let my self drift into a dream i would gladly lie
down on the soft sweet grass by the soft sweet her but i dont because if
i am in dreams then i am not here & i want to be here with her –

there is a tug on my string just as there is a tug on hers & together
we haul in our fish –

in that river there is tench dace roach bream etcetera so i dont know what my line has caught & as i pull it in i see the shimmer silver star sun under the water & know it is dace & i see another shimmer & know she has caught one too –

two small little dace enough for the suppers of four girls –

or two girls if we are allowed to eat the amounts we want which of course we are not –

it being better for a girl to be all ways a little hungry –

we haul in our fish & watch them flipflap & gispgasp on the grass –

we watch as their struggles start to slow & they start to give up –

& suddenly –

lets throw them back she says –

but then there will be nothing for supper i say except for peas & bread –

meat not being allowed that day because god says so –

well she says no one ever died from having just peas & bread did they –

& isnt it nicer –

isnt it better –

isnt it a strange sort of power –

to throw back the fish & watch them swim away –

yes i say –

if she had said let us make shoes of fish or let us build a house of fish or let us worship fish like they are god my reply would have been the same –

yes i say yes –

& so we do it –

we yank the hook from the fish & we throw them back into the water –

& we watch them swim away together –

scales shimmering in the dappling sun like some thing magical & secret –

///

i watch her writhe in her bed –

her back arching skin gleaming mouth open flipflap gispgasp –

i am not meant to watch i am only meant to clean the sweat from her brow & the vomit from her chin & the blood from her sheets –

she is not the first to be possessed by demons in this way & she wont be the last –

we girls are so open & leaky & full of holes & passages that we are easily entered by wickedness –

we have all been suffered this & we have all cleaned up the effects of each others suffering –

& it is never easy –

if i am honest it is easier to be the one possessed & demonridden because then at least you are the one making the mess & not the one cleaning it –

though when its her i dont mind the cleaning & i just want her to be comfortable until father fleck can get the demon out of her which it seems will take several days & so i am very attentive with my cloths & my buckets & i make sure the water is all ways fresh from the well & i pay attention to how much she vomits after father fleck forces his hands into her mouth to pull out the demon & i make sure i get enough bone broth into her to make up for what she has lost & i would like it if we could kill a calf or a lamb so i could take a little blood & give it to her to make up for what she has lost from the many small cuts & wounds on her arms & legs from the vigours of the exorcism –

though i know that bone broth will not make up for it –

i know that even all my blood would not make up for it –

though i would give it if i could –

well maybe not all of it because it is healthful to let some blood out but you mustnt take it all out & so i do need to keep some for myself –

but i do think i would have enough to share with her –

i wait until father fleck goes to his bed & i am alone with her & then i do a thing that my mother did for me when i was a child –

she made an ointment from poplar buds & black poppy & mandrake & henbane & vinegar & rancid oil –

but i dont have most of those things here at the sanctuary as i dont have the poison garden that my mother & i grew i only have the poppy & the oil so i make an ointment of them & i hope this is enough when i smear it across from one of her temples to the other & place a little too on her tongue –

& after that she sleeps for a while –

& i lie beside her & hold my hand to her throat to feel the throb there –

the next morning i am awake before father fleck returns & i wipe her face clean & i do think the ointment has done its work –

father fleck leans right over her in her bed so i can not see quite what he is doing –

but i can tell from the smells & the sounds it is the vomit & the blood just the same as yesterday –

i lurk in the door way with my clean water & my secret ointment & my heart in my mouth –

he pushes what looks like both his hands into her throat & pulls out a fist full of some thing that he throws into the slop bucket & i cant see any thing at all but that is why father fleck is holy & i am only a girl because he can see things that i can not –

he says as he goes out of the room with out looking back she is cleansed now –

lying there in her vomit & her blood & her tears she is cleansed –

father fleck leaves & it is just me & her i spend a long time with clean water & a clean cloth –

i do not know the hour because when we girls are beset by demons & have to be exorcised we are excused the usual church for matins & prime & terce & sext & none & vespers & compline & vigils –

so while the others are at their prayers & their cleansing i am doing a different sort of praying –

i only know it is late –

i only know i am tired –

i only know that finally she can rest –

& so i can too –

i lie down on my bed next to hers –

& i look at her sleeping face haloed holy in the candle light –

& i fall asleep in the glow of her –

///

there are things that i know –

that i know i am not supposed to know –

such as nettle can be pounded into plugs to stop a bloody nose –

such as black cohosh can bring on a mothers milk –

such as witch hazel can heal the tear in a womans most private place after the baby has come out –

such as foxglove will slow the heart & can be used to sleep a husband or a child no longer needed –

this last one is the one that people most often came to me & my mother to get –

not just foxglove but also narcissus & oleander & may apple & aconite & several other tinctures made from certain mushrooms & moulds –

but now i am here at the sanctuary i can not know these things –

even when i know they could help the other girls here with certain pains & ailments or even help the fathers who most of all must not know what i know –

which is quite fine as because i am a girl i am expected to know very little except catching fish & bringing in cows & picking peas & plucking chickens & baking bread & sweeping floors & making candles & collecting honey & making perfumes from flowers & dying cloth from plants & making boiled pigs face with cabbage in a particularly delicious way which now i think about it is actually quite a lot of things to know –

but any way these things are all i must know & no more –

no matter who asks –

the answer is no –

even if it is her & she needs me & i can help her –

the answer must be no –

///

all we girls are gathered –

me & jennet issobel beatrice matilda agnes gilleis lizabet petronella jehan hanna isidore oh & euphemia thats every one i think –

we are washing the sheets which is an unpleasant & lengthy task –

& father fleck says that is quite why we must do it because such girls as we need such tasks as this to make us holy –

or as holy as girls can be which as we all know is not very –

we are reddened & sweating & trying to think holy things –

& to distract us all she tells us about a mummer show that came to her village –

it was in the summer which is the time of dream bread –

where you are never sure whether the days food will give you strange visions or merely fill your belly –

some times in some years it does –

some times in some years it doesnt –

no one but god knows why –

she says she did have poppy seed bread that morning with her cup of mead & it was fortunate she had both of these as in summer some times there is no food to be had at all in that hungry time before the harvest –

which is when the mummer shows come through because they are hungry too & will perform any story that will lead to payment in food –

but she is sure this story was not from bread but was just as she saw it –

& i believe her because i know what it is to be hungry –

hungry for food & for stories & for the company of others & for colours & for sounds & for more more more –

even there at the sanctuary surrounded by my sisters & with the summer sun in my hair & so soon after we broke our fast i feel hungry in my belly & my eyes & my hands –

she tells us about the mummer show which was a story from the bible & so it was holy & healing to hear it –

adam & eve in the garden dressed in what looked like no thing at all –

but i think they must have been dressed in some thing they couldnt have been in front of every one in their bare skin so perhaps they had fleshings of white leather tight to their bodies so it looked like them selves that is all i can think & i suppose i do think on it slightly longer than i need to -

& she tells us up gobbled eve & the fruit -

& the fruit was some thing juicy & overripe so that its juice & wetness dripped & sprayed every where very messy very delicious its scent filling the air & making every one hungry & envious of eve in her wickedness -

& again i do think about that slightly longer than i need to -

& my belly & my eyes & my hands ache for the want of it -

& out came the devil & you knew it was the devil because he had - he had -

& here she can not tell the story any more her cheeks go pink & her hands go up over her eyes & i can not she says i can not say the words -

what i say what did the devil have -

& all the other girls look at me but i dont care i want to know how you know a devil when you see one -

a prick she says he had a prick -

like from a needle or a pin i say & i am thinking of a bead of blood on a finger tip -

no she says a prick like a man has -

but not like a real man would have or at least i think not because it is so big it is the length of a thigh & as wide as it too & all carved of wood so it goes thunk thunk thunk as he walks -

& by the way as she is telling me this she is still hiding her face in her hands & i can see her cheeks redden bright as rose petals & she peeks out at me to see if my cheeks are red too & i think they are -

so i look at euphemia & she is primly squeezing the water from a sheet as if she cares not for a prick no matter how big or how wooden which i dont think is true –

any way the devil & his prick went thunk thunk thunk across the stage & he bent over & let out a fart so fast & so stinking it must have been a wonder of contraption it was smoke & flames issuing from his back side & the stink of bad eggs –

& i wonder how they did that how they kept the bad egg stink in side & let it out only when they wanted perhaps a jar of some kind such are the wonders that exist in the world –

& i want to hear more about the flesh & the fruit & even the fart but i dont want to ask in front of the other girls as they are already looking at me too much & i know that curiosity is not proper for a girl –

so jennet tells a story about a man she heard of who was a jester to a great lord in a stronghold –

& the jester was so tall & so thin it was like he was already dead & bones –

& he was such a strenuous dancer he wore out 300 pairs of shoes in a single year –

& though i dont say it out loud it seems clear to me that the man was a thief & a liar –

that he was selling the perfectly good shoes & his silly master was providing more & more –

but i do not tell the other girls this because they did not grow up lying & stealing & tricking & poisoning & i do not want them to know that i did –

& some how jennet stops telling her story about shoes & we go back to the one about the mummer show –

because i will let you into a secret & that is none of the girls –

thats me & jennet issobel beatrice matilda agnes gilleis lizabet petronella jehan hanna isidore oh & euphemia –

what ever we might say to father fleck if he were to ask –

none of us are as interested in stories about shoes as we are in stories about pricks –

///

the next day the sermon is witches –

father fleck hears all the news from the living & from the dead as he speaks to travellers who pass through here & so he knows many things –

he tells us about a boy who said his mother was hiding two demons on a sheepskin bed in a secret place inside the roots of the crab apple tree & that she feeds them milk every day from a black plate –

he tells us about a man who had seven goats & one summer they started producing blood instead of milk & also his wife was with child but at the same time also lusty & he said both things were caused by the midwife who was ugly & widowed & had once cursed him when he would not pay her after his wifes last baby came out dead –

he tells us about a girl who bewitched another girl with unnatural lusts & they did unnatural things together such as only a husband & wife must do together –

he tells us about a woman who was cursed by a pedlar selling ribbons that she would not buy & he cursed her by saying she should have a red hot spit pressed to her buttocks & the next day her rear end & private parts were in a most strange & wonderful state –

he tells us about white lambs & black cats & tiny silken rabbits sent to do witches bidding in those dangerous hours when it is not quite night & not quite day –

all those witches were sent to burn which is the only thing to be done with them really –

father fleck says we are fortunate indeed to be in this place –

we must stay here at the sanctuary where we are safe –

so many things out there in the world are ready to curse us or hurt us or make us bleed or fill us with devils –

& i bow my head to pray & i think well what about the devils that fill us here –

what about the hurts we have here –

what about the blood that comes from us here –

but i suppose those things are different –

& i am still thinking about the girl & the girl & their unnatural marriage –

& if neither one had a prick then how did they lie like a man & wife –

a whittled nub perhaps –

a handle smoothed over many years of palms –

& i open my eyes just a little & i look over to her hands as she prays beside me –

& i look at her fingers which are pale & long & graceful & i think about the feel of them on my skin the feel of them on me & in me –

& i close my eyes tight & i press my palms together hard because no i will not think of that any more no i can not –

no –

///

yes i whisper in her ear when she comes for me at night –

i know then my reply to her will all ways be the same –

yes i say yes –

together we creep from our beds & go bare foot out onto the dew wet grass by the river –

we lie there letting it soak us to the skin –

we look up at the sky & she tells me how the stars are candles affixed on a faraway dome like the church roof only much bigger & much further away –

we lie there & watch those faraway candles flicker like fish –

i think of one of father flecks sermons about the difference between a man & a woman & how that difference can never be changed & we are born a way & that is how we are for ever & a man is a man & a woman is a woman & woman is for man & that is the proper way of the world & any thing else is witchrotten & devilridden & filth to the core of it –

& under the candle lit sky she comes close to me –

she leans close to me as if for a kiss –

but she doesnt kiss me –

she bares her teeth –

breath hot & tongue sweet & incisors smooth as silk –

& she bites me –

bites the line of my jaw –

bites me stills me holds me tight & soft with her teeth the way a mother cat holds a kitten –

the way a wolf holds a rabbit –

her mouth a trap her mouth a home her mouth a night sky i could fall into –

i think of how father fleck said that men have a need of light but women can live in darkness –

& there under the night sky with her hands in my hands & her mouth on my skin i dont see why that is a bad thing –

& i think if this is darkness then i will live here in the night with her for ever –

///

now i am the one possessed –

i am the one writhing & bloody –

the demon beclouds me in such a way that i hardly can tell his desires apart from mine –

some times when she is in my head –

he i mean he i mean the demon –

i can feel him inside me in my head in my heart in my in my in my –

i run through the sanctuary to our dormitory where the fathers do not go & i tear all my clothing & rip at the clothing & flesh of such of my sisters as i can lay hands on –

i trample them underfoot i chew them cursing the hour when i take the vows –

cursing the fish & the pond & the worms & our mercy our weak stupid mercy –

all this is done with great violence & i think i am not free & i know not what i do –

i know well that i do not do this thing by my own will but i also know to my great confusion that the demon can not have this power over me if i am not in willing league with him so i am to blame for allowing him into me –

& she comes to me then in the dormitory –

i want more than any thing to hear her voice so i close my ears –

i want more than any thing to touch her so i clasp my hands –

she takes my chin in her hand & tips my face to look at her –

i force my face away i can not look i can not –

i glare at her feet though i want more than any thing to look at her face –

she reaches for me & i look at her hands & i expect them to shimmer like fish scales –

to gleam in the low light like a secret magical thing from the sea –

i dont know why –

but when i look at her hands they are not secret they are not magical they are only hands –

///

matilda dies of a fever –

petronella falls to a visiting monk after creeping at night to his bed & he is gone again on his travels long before she knows a baby is coming & it is a long time before any of us knows because petronella is already round about the middle & is secretive about her monthly blood & when father fleck finds out she has to leave & i dont know that she ever finds that visiting monk or if the baby comes out alive or if petronella is alive –

beatrice is missing from her bed one day & we are told she ran away –

it rains & i think it has been raining for a while –

& i see now that it is not all ways summer –

it only seems that way because today is the same as the day before & the day after –

the world is just the same thing over & over –

new girls come grissel marion alizon & they are no different than the old girls no different than me we all pick the peas & pluck the chickens & get possessed by demons & the world is women in the dark & men in the light –

& that is gods way & the way it should be as father fleck says & i
should feel blessed for that –

because it wouldnt be good for it to be summer all ways –

summer is when we are hungriest & the bread tastes strange &
makes us see what is not there & makes us dream in the day & makes
us bite down on what is not good for us –

& makes us want –

& makes me want –

i can not want any thing –

i can not say any thing –

i can not know any thing –

& it is for the best –

i dont want to die of fever –

i dont want to be sent away –

i dont want to burn –

i only want –

i only want –

but theres no use in a girl wanting –

///

there are things i can not know –

but there are also things that others know & i dont –

such as every window is an eye –

every eye can see –

no thing is secret –

no thing is magical –

she is taken by a demon again & father fleck can not rid her of it –

she writhes & she cries & she bleeds & she calls for me –

she calls my name over & over & over & over –

i come with my cloths & my cool clean water & i never meet father
fleck eye –

& he never looks at me any way but this time he does –

because in her fever in her fits in her halfdreaming she calls to me –

& she speaks of the things that we did together –

father fleck listens he hears it all he sees it all –

when we went to the river with our hooks & our bait –

when we went to the river with our stars & our bites –

there is no thing secret now there is no thing magical –

there are only unnatural lusts –

there are only unnatural things –

there is only the fire & our flesh upon it –

& father fleck turns to me then –

as she writhes & she bleeds & she calls –

& he says to me there is no demon controlling her tongue –

there is no demon in side her making her sick making her burn –

some thing comes to her at night & brings a curse upon her & it is
not a demon & not a witch & not an incubus –

it is you –

yes i think but i dont say it –

she is in me as i am in her –

& he says to me did you know her sinful –

& he says to me did you lie with her evil –

& he says to me did you love her unholy –

i think of the fish we let go that day –

shimmering gleaming otherworldly –

& i know we didnt free it –

& i know it will just be caught tomorrow or tomorrow or tomorrow –

& it will die there gasping & writhing in the dirt –

but we gave it that day –

didnt we –

we gave it one more day to be free & that must count for some thing –

& he says to me do you love her –

do you –

do you –

no i say –

no –

Acknowledgements

I usually keep the acknowledgements to a simple list of names, but for this book I'm feeling chatty. 2024 is the year of my fortieth birthday, and ten years since my first book came out. Life sometimes gives you lovely synchronicities. If you count my Audible original, *The Sound at the End*, and the non-fiction book I share with Paul McQuade, *Hometown Tales: Glasgow* (which I do), this means that along with my three novels, three story collections and one memoir, *No & Other Love Stories* is my tenth book. Ten years, ten books. This wouldn't have been possible without the support, inspiration and cheerleading of many, many people.

Cathryn Summerhayes, the sort of agent every writer should have, who fights for me, advises me wisely (even when it's not what I want to hear), and tells me I'm a genius even though we both know all I do is make things up and write them down. You've helped me to sustain a writing career, which I've learned is even harder than getting a book published in the first place.

Liz Foley, I don't know how I got so lucky to have you as my editor. You push me to be better with everything I write, and you know what

ACKNOWLEDGEMENTS

I mean to say even when it's not what I managed to get on the page. You're excited to read whatever I write, no matter what it is. I know how rare that is, and I will never stop being grateful for it.

Bethan Jones and Mia Quibell-Smith, you are the most determined, tireless and generally excellent publicists I could have asked for. Here's to many glasses of wine at book festivals in the future.

Camilla Young and Katie Battcock, my film and TV agents. It's no exaggeration to say that you have changed my life in the past year. Your belief that I could write for screen made me believe it too.

Katherine Fry, you will always be my first choice for copy-editor. Your eagle eye and understanding of my style and voice is very precious to me. I think the hyphen clarification in 'fuckboy' vs 'fuck-toy' is my all-time favourite editorial note.

Kris Potter, for the sexy-creepy-tasty-gross cover design. I love it.

My books usually go through many rounds of edits and rewrites with my critique group, my agent and my editor – but not this one. I kept it close to my heart, dreaming the stories for a long time before I wrote them, and what you see on the page is almost exactly how they first emerged. While the content of the stories was very private, the process of writing them wasn't, and I had the company and support of many fellow writers while working on this book. They all continue to inspire me and make me envious of their enormous (and well-deserved) successes.

'Piglet', the story that sparked this whole collection, was written for Heather Parry at *Extra Teeth*, who told me to make it as weird as I wanted and not hold back. 'Unbury' started as the scrap of an image, and Lucy Rose's enthusiasm helped it grow; it was written in one morning at the Mitchell Library, sitting opposite Elle Nash. 'Linger' was written, again at the Mitchell, spurred on by the typing sounds and whirring brains of Rachelle Atalla and Cailean Steed. 'Devotion' was written for Rose Tomaszewska and Sarah Savitt at Virago, and the only reason I wrote that story and not one about cannibal mermaids was because Margaret Atwood stole the word 'siren' before I could start writing. 'Wreckage' was written for Ciara Elizabeth Smyth because she said it 'would make a spectacular TV show'. 'Trussed' was only half a story until Camilla Grudova brought deepfakes and Anna Walsh brought possession.

I found (and continue to find) solace and sustenance in several writerly WhatsApp groups, the content of which will remain secret to all our graves. Julia Armfield, Heather Parry, Alice Slater: one day we'll all go for drinks with Uncle Steve. Rachelle Atalla, Jessie Burton, Sophie Cameron, Imogen Hermes Gowar, Kiran Millwood Hargrave, Daisy Johnson, Hannah Kent, Lizzie McNeal, Anbara Salam, Nell Stevens, Francine Toon: bossing both parenthood and writing in the most inspirational and intimidating ways.

My family, too numerous to mention: all the Logans, Bennetts, Cairneys, Cooneys, Adairs, Jinkses and Sopers, I quite literally couldn't have written this book without you.

Annie, always. You support everything I do, you call me a gorgeous genius goddess, and you never let me believe my own bullshit. Every writer needs a Glasgow wife, and I'm glad you're mine.

And M, the reason for it all. I love you, I love you, I love you.

About the author

Kirsty Logan is an author of novels, short stories, chapbooks and collaborative projects with musicians and illustrators. She lives in Glasgow with her family, where she is working on film and TV projects.

@kirstylogan
www.kirstylogan.com